THE INTERCEPTOR

by

CHRIS CLOAKE

I dedicate this to all those who have shown genuine interest in my books. You are the buyers, readers and feedback givers. I hope what I have written this time will encourage you to stay with me for the journey.

With the help of my supportive family at home my working process is now well honed. I am confident a publication from me will now be an annual event. I use music and the words of other authors to inspire me. I played a lot of Springsteen. Those who are familiar with his songs and my writing will understand why. The amazing novels I have read this year are too numerous to list.

Love always to Sandra, Josh and George. You bring out the best parts of me and give back so much fun in the process. I am driven by the most important belief in the universe. The belief in oneself. Thank you again for giving that to me.

I'll see you all again – further on (up the road).

Chris Cloake September 2019

CHAPTER ONE

Carol couldn't understand a word the man was saying. His mouth was hardly moving, his glassy eyes were fixed on somewhere above their heads, as a stream of critical information poured out into the cold air.

She was sat on the benches that overlooked this bizarre ceremony, as near to the back as could be. Around her, everyone was male, and confident. They glanced at their brochures, watched the numbers get changed on the big board, nodded in understanding and exchanged the odd murmur of appreciation, or perhaps disgust, as progressive lots moved through.

Each time it was the same. A vehicle drove into the space below, the auctioneer launched into his garbled description, a few people twitched and appeared to be making bids and he banged his hammer down with a flourish. She was bewildered.

Carol reflected on her dilemma. No doubt if Marcus had been there he'd understand exactly what was happening and know how to get involved. Self assured bastard. As it was, she'd taken this on alone after watching someone on television at the hotel pick up an amazing bargain and have a lot of fun in the process.

"That's definitely a toupé," she said to herself, gazing at ridiculous chap leading proceedings.

"Are you all right, love?" came a voice beside her.

She turned to see an older guy with a weathered face, wearing a flat cap and a dubious expression.

"You seem a bit lost."

She assessed his interest and attempted to mirror his disdain. "No problems, thank you. I'm just waiting for the right one to come through."

3

He nodded like he barely believed her. She went back to the booklet she'd been handed when she came in. It was amazing how many there were for sale in only one morning.

"How you gonna choose which one is for you?" her new friend enquired.

She frowned at him, hoping that would be enough to shut him up. It wasn't. "I mean, being a woman and knowing nothing about cars. I guess you'll pick a colour you like and go with that."

She was taken aback for a moment. How rude! "I know what I'm looking for," she said, firmly. "I've registered and given a deposit."

He carried on as if his comment had been completely factual and not made to give offence. "Hard for you, though. As for me, I know what's a good catch from just a few details."

"Oh, really!" she huffed, and turned her attention back to the auction.

A nice red car was driven in and stopped in its shiny splendour. The auctioneer set off into his routine, pointing as his voice ascended and descended the scale. The price on the board was reasonable. Carol stuck her hand up like a school child to join in, only to find she was ignored. The hammer fell and it was all over.

The man beside her laughed. Carol clenched her fists and thought of Marcus. He would have treated her with the same mild amusement.

"Okay, Mister Know-it-all. What lot are you here for?"

"44. 1970 Jensen. Coming up soon. I'm ready for it, though I'll have to be smart."

Carol looked hurriedly at the list. There was a starting price set at £2500. That was more than she had intended to spend. But this was war now with this maddening misogynist beside her and she had to win. Defeat would only add credence to Marcus's parting words.

"You're a loser," he had spat.

"No, that me is in the past," she announced now. "I'll show you, you pathetic little man."

4

"What?"

She ignored him and watched carefully for the moment when Lot 44 was brought in. The babble and buzz around her faded as she tensed and fidgeted on her seat. Eyes clouding with tears and her body shaking, the success of her whole new start felt as if it would depend on these next few minutes.

"Be brave," she told herself.

The car that drew into the spotlight made her gasp. Long, slick, metallic blue with door handles, trim and wheel hubs glowing silver. The back was large and it tapered beautifully to the elegant bonnet. It oozed power and poise.

So taken was she with this vision, the process had begun before she regained her senses. The chap beside her was very involved, flicking his finger up regularly to counter others. The frenzied gabbling rose to a climax.

"I'm bidding!!" Carol shouted, standing up suddenly.

It seemed like the entire room closed in on her. Irritated and curious men turned around to see the source of this excessive interruption. The auctioneer managed to focus his contempt into a cold stare, his forehead wrinkling while his hairline remained fixed.

Carol could feel the blood pulsing in her neck while her head swam. She had to speak now or fall forever into a pit she couldn't run from.

"4000!" she exclaimed.

"Any advance on that?" was the call to the floor.

There was a pause of interminable length. Carol's legs wobbled. Silence prevailed.

"Sold! To the vocal lady there."

She flopped back down with a bump; the jolt released the breath she was holding.

"Hardly suitable for a woman!" the old man grumbled into her ear. She wasn't sure if he was referring to her outburst or the purchase.

"I guess," she replied, unsure of what had just happened.

"You did that on purpose. And way over value! I hope it was worth it!"

"Me too," she said, letting out a deep sigh.

CHAPTER TWO

There it was. Waiting for her. Gleaming, impressive and elegant, the world reflecting off the highly polished paintwork and silver trim. She owned this car. All the imagination that had gone into creating a dream of speed with sophistication belonged to a middle aged woman who had never handled anything larger than the family run-around.

She approached slowly, still feeling she was outside of an illusion, gazing in. It had all happened so quickly. An emotional release, motivated by impulse, demonstrative and not at all like her previously careful self. But that person was being left behind in the turning of the tide. The new Carol needed to emerge, at the wheel of this remarkable automobile.

The length of the bonnet alone was amazing. Carol ran her fingers along a line from headlight to windscreen, letting them flick against the grill on the top. She continued, all round the generous back to the other side, a first light touch of a love she was sure would blossom.

The soft roof had a patch in the centre. She realised this would likely fold back. She knew then she could look forward to some great sensations on the endless roads, with the top open and the surge of a huge engine pulling her forwards.

When she put the key in the door she hesitated, as if there might be some possibility of turning back. Of course, there wasn't. They were destined to be together now. This was her saviour, come to lead her to the next phase of life.

What she intended to be a purposeful entry became clumsy as she fell into the big, bucket of a driver's seat. The red leather was finely cracked and cold against her palms when she planted them down to steady her drop. "Whoah!" she cried.

She stretched out her legs but they didn't reach the pedals. She did the same with her arms and could only just touch the steering wheel. Leaning manically out, she pulled the big door shut. The aroma of the interior was now strong, kind of dusty and oily, and reassuring like the sideboard in her parents' lounge.

Below her left elbow a large boxed panel held the gear stick and lots of controls. A set of dials faced her through and beside the wheel. The milometer read 39648. There was a lot of car here, ready to spring to life at her control. She laughed out loud, through amazement and anxiety.

"Am I really here?" she asked.

A glance into the rear view mirror confirmed her suspicions. She twisted it to see herself better. Was the short hair a good idea? It showed more of her face, which was bony, and her skin, which was stretched with lines. The trip to the hairdressers had coincided with the decree absolute coming through; a time for renewal.

Her eyes were the same, she thought, washed out grey. And in their depths the uncertainty and need to please still lurked, threatening to diminish her every effort to move on. And she could see that patch of chest skin flushing red as it always did when she was stressed. She would scratch and tear at it until a rash developed. And why wear that twee, spotty blouse with the oversize collar?

"What would Marcus say now?" she wondered. "Ridiculous," she decided. "And my friends? How they've dwindled since my need increased. They'd likely tell me to get real."

Her reflection looked unhappy.

"So how about Richie? He might be excited. He's eleven after all and loves the motor racing."

Then his snarl of disappointment loomed in her mind. He believed his dad went because she had been so boring. Now it was too late. She sighed. The world continued to offer plenty of challenges.

She gazed out, along a vast bonnet that went up from the windscreen to a peak in the centre. Beneath this immense hood lay the power, formidable enough to take her far away. But to where? All she had right now was the desire to go. She would drive back to the hotel and make proper plans. There was going to be somewhere she could make a fresh start, out of the city and the awful, tired group of acquaintances.

"To do that, I need to start her up," she said.

Gripping the steering wheel and the chair lever together, she shot herself forward enough to reach the pedals. On the turn of the key, she expected a sluggish response. An immense, earthy roar was released, shaking the interior. A bird flew off from the tree beside her, leaving in its wake a scattering of orange leaves.

The engine settled into a solid rumble that promised much more. Life had been unleashed. She switched the radio on too. The urgent voice of Tom Robinson soon blared from the speakers, raging like a fire around her.

"2-4-6-8."

The effect was energising. This was a new song for a new era. Once, she would have turned the sound right down. Now, her ears sung with the release and her blood surged. With childish mirth, she pressed a button and the window went down in erratic jolts. Her smile was irrepressible.

She caressed the surfaces, black plastic designed to feel like smooth leather, an inlay of highly polished wood, all finished with shiny metal. It gave an impression of solidity. Perseverance that held a history.

"So who did you serve before me?" she wondered.

The description had indicated careful ownership. As if it would ever describe the previous keeper as slapdash! Even so, it seemed very well loved. Having made no effort to see the vehicle before she bought it, she was fortunate. This was a lucky day.

She scanned the dashboard. A few needles flickered while she gently lowered her foot on the accelerator and increased the revs.

"This is what those idiots always do on their motorbikes," she said. "It sounds good when you are the one in control."

9

She felt the vibration penetrate through her backside, sending a delicious tingle upwards until tummy, spine and chest sang in delightful unison. Overcome by the sensation, she laid her cheek on the wheel.

It was then she noticed a very definite dent in the dashboard on the passenger side. Something had hit this spot with force. She sat back and saw everything differently. Those air vents were whispering a tale from the past. The head rest she pressed into held the impression of someone else. She could see where the pedals were worn. What story could this car tell?

CHAPTER THREE

Greg Jackson bought a brand new Jensen Interceptor on 2nd February 1970. It was just the right car for him. Or so he thought. Showy, with a price that spoke of wealth and a realised ambition. People would respect him now he had an emblem of status to drive around and share.

Most of his acquaintances, the low lifes and middle men of petty crime and shady deals, quietly regarded the car as an extravagance he could ill afford. A failed attempt at class where none existed. Those closer to home were more vocal.

"What a waste of money," his wife declared when he arrived wearing his stupid lopsided grin and waving the keys in her face.

"Val, you don't get it. I deal in fine jewellery. If you gonna buy a watch from me I need to look affluent."

"The Morris Minor was fine."

A look of consternation twisted his wiry features. "You gotta be joking! It was stupid. Now I can carry on my business and be believed."

She sagged against the door as she lost the strength to stand. He was pitiful. The stripy suit, high polished shoes and hair swept into a ponytail did nothing to hide the foolishness. It was her foolishness. Caught off guard one boozy New Years Eve twelve years ago when five minutes of madness behind the bins down the side of the pub had left her pregnant and linked to him forever. And each time he returned she was reminded of the depth of her recklessness. Now she guarded her threshold more stoically.

"Where's my welcome?" he demanded. "I've been away working hard. Haven't you even got a kiss for me?"

"It's five months since I last heard a thing from you," Val countered, the lines on her brow deepening.

His glassy blue eyes flicked about, searching for an answer. "That long?" he said.

11

"Don't try and act surprised. You're always doing it."

The moment settled into an impasse. A cocky chap who sported a moustache to try and appear older and a tired girl whose white complexion, lank locks and air of foreboding spoke of how she had lost her sparkle and a budding career as a nurse. He was incapable of thinking of an excuse and she had no power to push him away because of their son.

"How's Chad?" he asked, as if reading her thoughts.

She gritted her teeth. "Fine, as if you care."

"I do!" he protested, coming up the steps to the door. "Let me see him."

"He's at school you prick."

"Well, I'll come in and wait. I've got a present for the little rascal."

"He doesn't want anything from you," she spat, wishing this wasn't such a lie.

"Can't I just see him?" he pleaded, reaching forward.

He laid his right hand, with its red birth mark that looked like a sore, on her shoulder. "Let us in, I'm so very cold out here."

He wore a large, jewelled skull ring. A showy symbol of everything he was. His masculinity flowed through it, the energy he generated for his devious little life. She could feel his thumb caressing her neck. She shut her eyes. The touch of a man was so rare for her. Thus began her surrender again. The pattern would repeat. He'd stay a few days, spoil Chad with money and attention, show her some ardour she told herself was love, then be gone.

"You seem a bit tired," he said.

"What do expect? Bringing up a boy on your own."

"I'll take you out, make you feel special." He slid his rakish frame into the hall. His lemony cologne was strong. "You ain't going to cry again are you?"

"I've no tears left," she sighed, and led him upstairs to the flat.

~

"Mummy, I'm home!"

12

Chad's voice from the hall made the muscles in her shoulders tighten. She heard him drop his bag and shoes off with a thud before coming into their lounge to encounter the unexpected vision of his dad. He instantly grinned uncontrollably and then threw a glance at his mother. She was standing off to the side, clutching herself tightly.

Those persuasive blue eyes of his sought her approval to be happy about his dad's arrival. She saw Greg in them. They were his eyes. But unlike his father he also perceived her pain. He heard her crying sometimes, noticed her struggles, helped her count the coins to see if they had enough to last the week.

She gestured with her head for him to get on with it and walked from the room into the kitchen. It wasn't far enough away to escape the sound of Greg's manipulation of the boy. She hated what he did, making him feel precious, remarking on his growth and throwing promises that would never get kept.

"Fucking bastard!" she hissed.

What hurt most was the knowledge that she was just as susceptible to his wolf like charms. She threw a plate into the sink so hard it shattered.

Letting the anger out was the only way of staying sane. She continued with the chores, making noise to drown out their laughter.

"Mummy, that car outside is daddy's!" Chad exclaimed, appearing beside her and jumping up and down on the spot.

"Yes, I know," she replied.

"He's going to take me for a drive!"

"Oh, is he?"

"Now."

"Now? Your tea will be ready and you have homework to do."

"Pleeeeease, mum. I can't wait!"

She gave him a troubled look which he returned with lips pursed into a kiss.

13

"I guess you better get on with it. He won't be here long so you don't want to miss out."

"He says he's staying this time."

Seeing Chad's eyes twinkling with expectation, his energy surging, pierced her heart. She ruffled his hair.

"Go on big guy."

He hugged her, a touch of reassurance before heading off for his adventure. Now her tears came and she smacked her own thigh with the tea towel in frustration. When Greg stepped in she turned away to face the bland city rooftops. He saw her stooped over the sink, her frayed strands of hair appeared grey in the light from the window.

"We'll just go for a spin along by the river," he said.

"Whatever."

She had hunched her shoulders in obvious displeasure. He sought an easy solution.

"Come with us," he suggested.

"I don't think so," she retorted, the malice clear in her voice.

"You could try and enjoy yourself," he continued.

Now she faced him, hands on hips, and despite her diminutive stature, he stepped back.

"That boy is all I have in this lousy world that matters. I've got a crummy job, parents that disowned me for being a slut, I feel crap, look crap, have no money, no pride and no hope. I don't want to share him with anyone, least of all a long term no hoper. He's the only thing of any goodness to ever come from you.

"So don't tell me to be happy. You can go have your bit of fun if it makes you feel like a man or even a father. Treat him well and then go back to the disdain. Every time it gets harder to take. So fuck off and make sure you get him home by six because we have to do normal, boring stuff you wouldn't know about."

14

He twitched uncomfortably. "I can be part of the family," he protested, more out of defence than sincerity.

"You'd need to become part of the human race first, and I can't see that happening."

His laugh ran out of steam half way through when he realised she wasn't making a joke. He turned stiffly and left.

She watched them through the net curtains at the front, smiled at Chad's mad gestures of delight before tasting the bitterness of envy when they raced off, the shimmering blue of the car lighting up the drabness of her street.

~

"Aaaaiiiigh!!!!!!" Chad wailed as Greg eased the car through the gears. Greg's hands tightened on the steering wheel. The ruby in the skull of the large gold ring he wore glinted in the light. Greg assumed a god like status. They went far too fast for the road. Chad could hardly hold himself up in the front seat high enough to see down the bonnet. An old man on a bicycle tumbled to the side as they roared past.

"Silly sod!" Greg shouted. "Get some real wheels!"

"I love this, dad!"

Greg smiled to himself. "Every boy loves speed."

When they had to stop at a pedestrian crossing, Greg rattled his fingers on the wheel impatiently. A girl in very short skirt walked by and Greg revved the engine in appreciation.

"And every boy notices a nice bit of arse," he added.

Chad giggled. Mummy didn't use language like that. The release was refreshing. Life at home was hard with so many things he couldn't do. Mum was wired to only see the hazards. It was as if she wanted to protect him from every possible mistake. That could never work.

They turned onto an old dockyard thoroughfare, deserted except for some old rubbish bins with signs up warning of a dead end.

"Now let's rip," Greg growled.

Chad held his chin up and watched the disused buildings and old cranes whizzing by against the concrete sky.

"You can get places with motor like this," Greg told him.

"And arrive early!" Chad agreed.

Greg laughed. "That's the spirit."

Chad gripped the smooth leather of the seat and wondered what all the dials on the dashboard actually meant. This wasn't like other cars he had been in. His friend's mum had a silly little square thing that felt empty inside. It made a clattering noise when she changed gear and she shouted 'fuck!' every time and made them smirk in the back seat.

The Jensen to Chad was something else. Full of purpose. Every piece was designed to increase the speed and make it look ready for racing. There was order and wildness rolled into one. Actors and pop stars drove this kind of machine. He wanted to be seen by everyone he knew.

"Shall we do something cool?" his dad asked.

"Yeah!"

"Dangerous and cool?"

"And fun!"

Reaching a large open area bordered by rusty railings, Greg yanked the handbrake on and turned them right around to face the other way. As the car rocked to a standstill, Chad whacked his elbow on the door. He winced with pain.

"You hurt?" Greg asked.

"No," Chad lied.

They looked at each other and burst into a mutual whoop of delight.

"That was amazing!" Chad yelled.

"Shall we do it again?"

"Yes, yes!"

While Greg took the car round in readiness for another go, Chad clutched his hands together. "I'm gonna dream about this tonight."

"Good," Greg said.

After another thrilling spin, Chad demanded more. Greg considered his large, shiny, watch and shook his head.

"We're already over time. We have to get back to your mom."

"She'll be okay, I can win her over."

"Maybe. But I'll need to be in her good books too or she won't let me stay."

"Okay," Chad agreed, immediately.

While they drove home, Greg glanced at the little boy beside him and thought he looked too thin and weedy. There was too much neck. His limbs were all angular and awkward. It was a sweet face you could never distrust but more resilience was needed. He still had a lot of growing up to do.

"What you have to do is use people in the right way to get what you want. Don't be pushed around or kicked down. Work out the best way to achieve your goals and concentrate on that alone. Everyone else you can make fit in."

Chad thought for a moment. "Even those that you love, like mummy?"

"Yes, even mummy."

~

It was Christmas Day when Greg came again. He bore the inevitable gifts of the guilty. She had so wanted to leave him out on the doorstep with the snow collecting on his stupid peaked hat. She softened just as the city had as a peaceful hush descended on the world for those brief, magical hours.

"Action Man, with real hair!" Chad exclaimed "And his tank!" he continued, tearing the paper from another present. "Thanks, daddy!"

"What a great father you are," she said sarcastically once Chad had disappeared along to his room with his new prize.

"I didn't forget," Greg mumbled, sitting down opposite.

"Except for the last ten months!"

17

He shrugged. "I've been, well, busy."

She stared at him. Unable to lock eyes with her, he fiddled with a bauble on the tree beside him.

"He's not been that well," she informed him. "His asthma plays up."

"Never knew he had it," was the reply.

"Well, why would you?"

"He needs to get out more, man up a bit."

Val sighed and took a deep breath. "He built a snowman in the park yesterday."

"Cool."

"He might have liked to do that with you."

"Can't be helped." He sniffed and rubbed his hands together. "Shall I put the fire on, it's bloody chilly in here."

"We're saving it to later. We can only afford heat in the evenings."

"I'll give you some cash," he decided, leaning over to flick the switch.

The smell of burning dust filled the small room. He glanced around. Most of the decorations were home made. He thought it looked cheap and nasty but kept that to himself.

"Aren't you going to open your present?" he asked.

She looked down at it sitting there by her feet, all shiny with an oversized purple ribbon perched on top. "What's the point, it won't be anything useful."

"Go on," he urged, grinning enough to reveal his gold tooth.

She went through the ritual with zero enthusiasm. Inside was a silky red box which, as she lifted the lid, revealed a beautiful diamond studded necklace. She observed it coldly.

"Well, do you like it?" he enquired, crouching forward.

"It's stunning," she admitted, touching it lightly for a moment.

"Good," he said. She put it to one side. "Ain't you gonna try it on?"

"Why bother? I'll never wear it."

"Why not?"

"Firstly, I never go anywhere that warrants jewellery despite your promises to take me out and second, I know everything you acquire is stolen."

He pushed his chin down in a gesture of hurt. "Not true. I paid a packet for that."

"Then you wasted your precious money," she said, getting up.

"Can't you just put it on today?" he pleaded.

"To wear with this?" she demanded, throwing out her hands to emphasise a sweatshirt and jeans that had seen a lot of use. "This is my best stuff."

"I shoulda got you a dress too," Greg concluded.

"No Greg. It would take a lot more than one dress. I've got bags under my eyes at thirty two, skin like sandpaper and—"

"Your hair looks nice," he cut in. "I love it long."

"It's only got that way because I can't afford the cuts."

"Been tough has it?"

"Funnily enough, the laundrette didn't give us staff a Christmas bonus this year."

"Oh," was all he could muster as a response. He hadn't a clue where she worked.

She clenched her fists and growled in frustration. "I'm going to make the dinner."

"Good, I'm starving," he said.

She turned and considered slapping his face. He reached out and helped himself to a chocolate from the packet beside the chair. She dived down and snatched them away.

"Those are our treat. They've got to last us."

"I can get you a whole load."

"No thanks, Greg. Save your dirty money for yourself."

He walked up to where she stood, clutching her cherished box like a shield. She looked up in defiance. He had never physically hurt her. All of her scars were in the heart. He bent down and kissed her undefended lips. "Merry Christmas, my love."

~

"Grown again?" Greg exclaimed when he returned at Easter.

He put his hand up from where he sat and patted Chad on the head. Chad stood still and waited for the inevitable present. None came.

"Thin with it though," his dad continued, gripping one of his arms with a vice like palm. "School going okay?"

"Yeah, mostly," Chad replied, though there was a hesitation.

"He's been getting bullied," Val cut in from her viewpoint at the door.

"What?" Greg snapped, his interest suddenly acute.

Chad shuffled on the spot, his head hung low.

"Who's doing that to ya?"

"Some bigger kids," he muttered.

"Well, you gotta stand up to them. Give back a bit of their own medicine." Val was twitching with agitation. "Really, Greg, these boys are fifteen. What chance do you think he'd have against them?"

Greg remained indignant. "It's when the odds are thin you have to stand up and win," he insisted, smirking at his accidental bit of poetry.

"And you'll be here to patch him up when he comes home, will you?"

Val's barb made him waver in his lecture. He collected his thoughts while poor Chad twisted back and forth, looking for guidance from both parents.

"We gotta toughen you up, Chad," he said, taking a look around the room. "Not in here, it's too pokey. We'll go out to the park and get working on it."

Val followed them. The sun was strong as it streamed through branches not yet in leaf. Beneath the solid boughs she watched Greg crouch down in front of Chad, take off his jacket and urge him to punch his outstretched palms over and over again. He pushed him on until Chad collapsed on the grass, gasping for breath.

"Enough of this," Val ordered, stepping forward.

"He has to keep on, when he can't give no more, he has to do more."

"It's not the answer."

"What's yours?"

"I've spoken to the boys' mothers."

Greg face tightened in distaste. "That's no good. I better it didn't work."

Val offered no answer.

"Right. It didn't."

"I want to talk to the school."

"No!" Chad shouted from the ground.

Greg threw his hands out in an irritating gesture that he considered enough to prove his judgment was sound.

"Can we go for a drive after?" Chad asked him.

"Sure thing, buddy."

Val squeezed her forehead as if trying to force the scene from her head.

Greg's smile betrayed him. He loved winning like this. "So, we go again, Chad. Hit as hard as you can."

"I can't watch," Val announced.

"Then why are you?" Greg retorted.

"Protecting him against your mad scheme."

Chad stopped. "Mum, I'm fine. I want to do this. I'll see you back at home."

Val was reluctant to leave them. Chad's china blue stare cut through her resolve. Feeling like a stranger spying on someone else's family, she returned to the flat and filled her pillow with helpless tears.

CHAPTER FOUR

Chad had to wait over two years for the chance to share with his father the success of the new approach he had taught him. After a couple of initial beatings, Chad's day came when he stood at the top of the hierarchical tree and punishments were dished out to the weak.

"I don't recognise you anymore," Val complained, after she'd received another call from the school detailing his bad behaviour.

She had to follow him to his room when he refused to answer her flurry of questions. He sat at the desk where he once did his homework and met her pleas with a solid stare via the mirror before him. His face had developed the same hard edges of his frame, which was stretched out and twitching as he lay back in the chair.

"All this hardness is fake," she said.

"It's my only hope in this shithole neighbourhood."

"You were once such a sweet little boy."

He considered the diminutive frame of his mother that hung from his door, her small jaw and that thin little neck he had sought solace against when the world was being cruel. She represented safety and home. A place he might come back to for a rest from the battle. But her perpetually dull brown and grey clothes and the tiny horizons she didn't dare cross would not help to keep the two of them close.

"Save your strength for yourself," he told her. "We all need to be tough to survive."

"You don't need to shut your feelings away. You're still my son and I know you love me."

"I have to be like this. I get it from dad. My past is painful, so poor and pathetic. I need to leave that me behind."

22

Val shut the door to hide the sting of his words. Despite all her focusing on the bright and better aspects of their life, Greg had seeped in through the cracks she could not paper over and twisted this boy's soul. She was losing her only child, being cast adrift from her own story.

Hearing a bang on the door, she let her drooping shoulders take her down to answer it. Most days brought something bad, someone wanting money. This particular one turned out to be exceptionally so when she saw Greg's chilling frame step into the hallway.

He was very keen to get inside, even by his wormy standards. He looked back out, up and down the street, before he spoke.

"I'm staying here a while," he informed her.

"Do I get any choice?"

He finally let his flickering eyes notice her reaction. "You can't turn me out?"

"I want to. I thought you might be dead, it's been so long. I see that wish hasn't been fulfilled."

He stretched his arms towards her, the red patch on the hand like an open wound. "Val. Let's not argue. I need you more than ever."

"The feeling isn't mutual."

"I've been let down by a contact. Now my head's on the block." He sniffed. "I parked the Jensen a few streets away. If I disappear for a few days, the heat will drop. I'll be in the clear."

"Well disappearing is what you've always been good at. Do you know how long it is since you last saw us?"

"A year nearly?"

"Fourteen months," stated Chad, as he strode down the stairs.

"Chad, my son!" Greg called.

This time Chad showed no pleasure at his father's arrival. The hard new lines of his teenage face did not alter. He had both hands plunged in his jean pockets and stiff limbs.

"Did I miss your call?" Chad demanded. "Somehow mum affords a phone. How hard would it have been to ring up and see how we are?"

Greg had backed away, now trapped between a hostile outside world and a growing child who had finally rumbled him.

"I....well....I....meant to."

Chad kept on coming. He was the same height as Greg now. Val held her breath. Chad stopped, glanced up and down at Greg's suit and shoes that had obviously seen better days, sniffed the acidic cologne that hung in the air and then shook his head.

"Not even a sorry. If mum let's you stay, that's her business. As for me, I'll keep to my room. I don't want to spend a single minute with you."

Val looked at Greg as Chad walked away. In the poor electric light his skin was sickly and sallow and he merged with the pasty yellow wallpaper of the hallway. His jaw twitched uncomfortably. His eyes were cast down at the threadbare carpet, unable to meet his son's eye.

"What's got into him?" he asked.

"You, Greg," she said, with a smile.

~

"Where's the jewellery I've given you?" Greg demanded.

Val was watching her favourite television programme and was in no mood to talk to him. Being ignored, he fidgeted on the spot, glancing from the screen to her.

"Well?"

Val frowned. "Well, what?"

"The stuff I've bought. You've still got it, right?"

"I sold it at the market," she said.

"Fuck!" he screeched. "They were gifts!"

"Meaningless ones," she reminded him.

"To you maybe!"

"Oh, don't be stupid. I was winding you up."

24

She laughed as his juvenile expression went from hurt to angry. He wanted to storm off but knew he needed to persevere. Her ongoing chortling had to be disregarded.

"Can you get it for me?" he continued.

"I'm watching this!" Val hissed.

Forced to sit and wait, he sank into his chair and kicked the coffee table over. No amount of growling or sighing would make Val respond to the pressure. This rare bit of control over him was a sweet victory. Only when she was ready, she got up, and went into her bedroom, returning with an old shoebox.

"There," she said, throwing it onto his lap.

"You keep it in this?"

"To match the worth of the contents."

"Ah, that's where you're wrong," Greg said, his thin lips turning up into a wicked smile. "These jewels are my saviour."

He picked through the pile within, disentangling necklaces and bracelets with more tenderness than she had ever seen from him.

"So you don't want any of this, right?"

She'd known where this was leading. The pause that followed was engineered by her to increase Greg's suffering.

"I need some loot to save my skin," he bleated.

His attempt for sympathy with appealing eyes and quivering chin was an insult to her intelligence. She cared no more for him than he had that night at the pub when her young face had said yes in the swell of the crowd. The wrinkles she developed in the years since served to underline that fact.

"Take them."

"Val, you're a star!"

He launched himself across to her seat. She shielded him off with bony forearms.

25

"Don't even try to thank me. I hate them more than you. They remind me of my mistake."

He was on his knees in before her, which she found vaguely pleasing. "I'll get you some more," he assured her.

"Please don't bother."

He reached out and put his heavy ring hand on her thigh. She brushed it off like it was dust.

"It's good to be here with you, Val," he purred in a loathsome soft tone.

"Rubbish. You're using us a bolthole. A last resort. I think you're pathetic and so does Chad. Now if you'd return to the kitchen. I've got something else I'm going to watch. And stand that table back up as you go out."

~

Chad walked hunched with head down and hands deep in pockets, grimacing against the ill wind that blew between the concrete walls of his estate. He pulled his eyes from the broken paving slabs when he heard the earthy growl of a powerful car engine starting up. Sure enough, it was his dad's Jensen.

That sound clouded his memories, it was the signal for him to be left behind, the roar of rejection. Chad shook his head in confusion. Some of the best moments of his life had been spent in that car and yet it had come to represent a dead weight tied to his ankle.

He slowed down and huddled lower, electing to pass by unnoticed. No such luck.

Chad had always thought it was so cool that the windows went down at the press of a button. Now he cringed at the flash gesture as Greg leaned across to get his attention.

"Chad, my boy, glad I got to see you before I left."

"Going already then?" Chad retorted.

"It's been five days."

"Just long enough to bomb mum's world again."

Chad walked on, Greg matched his pace, the car purring as it rolled along next to the curb.

"I'd liked to have some time to catch up with you," Greg called. "I hear your tough guy routine is knocking them dead. It must have been so satisfying to see their frightened faces."

"I survive," Chad said, fixing his gaze ahead. "On my own."

"We all have to," Greg agreed.

"Some have dads who offer support."

"I'll be back sooner this time."

Now Chad stopped. He looked deep into the core of his father and saw only a blank space. "You won't," he concluded.

His son's new sharpness cut through his act so easily and beyond this he had nothing to offer. He twisted in the big red leather driver's seat and found himself wishing he had gone without a word. Chad sensed the discomfort and found a tiny drop of sentiment rise to the surface.

"Why don't you ever stay?" Chad asked.

Greg breathed in deeply. "I gotta keep moving in my job. Staying in one place would make me lose business."

"You could come home more often."

"Maybe." Greg shrugged. "I just don't need people. Arms around me feel like a trap."

"So it's easy to leave?"

"If you don't get too involved, it can't hurt you much."

"Well there's no chance of that!"

"I'll be back," Greg assured him. "We can talk better then. We used to have lots to say."

"Once. Never again."

As Chad walked away down his street, he was full of hate. Hate for his father and the complete nothing he ever got from him. And hate for himself.

Because even in this moment he realised that his growing emotional detachment was a direct emulation of the man he had just rebuked.

~

Before the rumble of the Jensen had faded, Chad could hear his mother crying. He found her crumbled against the faded wallpaper in the hall, head on her knee. She rarely showed this amount of distress. Chad felt uncertain.

"It can't be that bad," he ventured. "He's fled like this ever since you met him."

"He's stolen my money!" she wailed.

"How much?"

"Two hundred pounds. I had it hidden in granny's teapot. He must taken it while I was at work."

"What a bastard!"

She might have admonished him for his language had he not been so accurate.

"You left him alone in the house with that amount of dosh?" Chad said.

Val raised her clouded eyes and saw him shaking his head in disbelief. The sympathy she needed wasn't going to come from him.

"Great!" he scoffed. "We'll be eating shit for weeks! How could you be so dumb?"

"I never thought he'd stoop so low."

"Filth always sinks to the bottom," Chad said, walking past the heap of his mother and seeking the solitary solace in his room.

~

In September 1976, the cloud that was Greg fell over them again. Three years without seeing him did not dilute the bitterness. Val was resolute. With arms sternly folded, she backed him away from the front door and out onto the pavement.

"You're not coming in, Greg," she said, as if it wasn't already obvious.

28

This time Greg had lost all of his customary swagger, the stupid ring and the tailored suit. He was plain and pallid, like her. His hair hung down, lank with grease, and he had grown an uneven, wispy beard. He needed some tender female care that would have come naturally to her if she hadn't been filled with such loathing.

"Not even for a while?" he suggested.

"I can't. Chad has sworn he will knock you through the wall if he ever sees you again."

Greg glanced up at the windows above, a haunted, hunted look on his face. Val had waited for this moment for a long time. And yet she still managed to raise her own temperature to boiling. "I should have you arrested, you thief!"

"It was just a bit of cash! I'll see you right soon enough!"

"Just go away, Greg, and leave us alone. For good."

"I brought the boy a gift," he countered.

"He's not a boy now. Those days are gone. We're tired of your empty gestures," she said. "No more."

Val put all the weight she could muster into a push. A push of hate. A push of finality. Greg was taken by surprise, staggered, but managed to keep his balance.

"I'm giving him the car!" he protested, gesturing to the sleek motor parked behind him.

"Don't be daft."

"I am. I've done the paperwork, look!"

While he pulled out some green paper from his pocket, she checked to make sure Chad hadn't heard them. She snatched the document from Greg's hand and stepped away to read it carefully. Quickly, she saw that he was, on the surface, telling the truth.

"I can't believe you were ever the legal owner."

Greg's pained reaction would have been comical if she hadn't hated him so much. "I bought that new," he screeched.

"There's one of your tricks behind this," she concluded.

He came to stand beside her. She stepped away.

"No, honest. I want him to have it. He always used to love our spins. He must be old enough now, yes?"

"He's eighteen in a week. You should know that, of course."

"Well, I did," he fibbed.

"Not," Val said.

"All the same, what a great time for him to get a car. And what a car!"

Val thrust the paper back to him. "You can't do this. I have a strong idea you're going to need some collateral in the near future."

"I can always make a buck," he argued, ignoring her gesture.

"We've had debt collectors calling for you here."

"Here? How did they get the address?"

"It matters not. When they came first, Chad was on his own. They were big buggers, mean as shit. He got quite upset, telling me about it. He thought we might lose the flat, so I explained it was the Council's property and nothing to do with you."

Greg was not interested in any distress he might have caused. His mind was racing with this new information. Scanning the area around him he became very eager to leave.

"Here, take the keys!"

He planted them into Val's palm. A tussle ensued, each of them trying to empty their hand. Greg was stronger and Val ended up against the railings, twisted at an odd angle, her tight features straining.

"Listen," Greg hissed. "If I sign the car over to him, it means I won't lose it to that scum. I'd hate them to get hold of my beauty and I can't pay them what I don't have."

"So you'll take the thing back once you're out of trouble," she said, meeting his glassy eyes as she had so often in the past and finding them lacking resolve.

He shrugged. "Who knows. I've got to lay low for quite a while to get out of this one."

"I'm right."

Still she stared him down, their foreheads pressed together. He'd lost his usual light, acidic aroma. It was replaced by the whiff of sweat she found hard to endure. He was hurting her back and she winced, but held on. Eventually, he relented and she could stand up and become separate from him again.

"He'd love that car. You're heartless," he complained.

"I'm heartless?"

Val laughed despite her aching lungs. He felt the frustration rising. In his time, he'd negotiated his way through tough deals and bluffed dangerous dealers. When it came to women and the emotions they stirred, he was hopeless. This was one of the many reasons he limited his time with them. Val sensed victory and liked how it destroyed his cocky demeanour "Well, tough guy. What are you going to do now?"

Greg heard in Val's callous tone all the unhappiness he had caused. That cute little thing he had taken behind the bins that night was now a venomous dwarf. He wanted to hit out at a world he could no longer control.

"Fuck off!" he shouted and threw the keys at the house, where they landed with a clank at the bottom of the steps.

Before Val could reach them, Chad appeared and picked them up. He turned them over in his hand and then looked up to see Greg hurrying away towards the underground station, leaving the parked Jensen behind.

"I heard shouting. I should have guessed it was him."

Val held out her hand. "Give me those," she demanded.

31

Chad shook his head. "He's left his precious motor behind. We can borrow it like he borrowed that money."

"You'll not do anything of the sort," she continued.

"But I have the key and you don't."

He held his hand up high and laughed while she tried to jump to reach it, teasing her with many near misses. She struggled on for a while before becoming breathless. She aimed a punch at his ribs and met only solid muscle under his tight t-shirt. His hours at the gym had paid off, he was surprisingly solid now. She sagged, hands on thighs, her head level with his knees.

"Really, Chad. You can't even drive."

"I reckon I know enough. It'll be fun."

She had not seen him smile this much in many a year. What a shame it was for all the wrong reasons. He would always be that melodic chime that had stirred her love from the moment she first held him as a baby. She only ever wanted him to be happy.

"You haven't got to climb in it right away. He's given it to you."

"Never!" he exclaimed with rare passion. His eyes narrowed on the car. "I'm not stupid. He'll be back soon enough, and he'll take it away again."

Val stretched up to her not very full height. "Not this time. Sounds like he's in a real fix. And he knows the debt collectors have traced him here. I understand your father well enough. He'll be gone for ages."

She saw a moment's hesitation sneak across his adolescent face and stole in to take advantage, pressing herself against his firm frame.

"Listen, Chad. I'd rather we just sold the thing and booked us a holiday, a nice trip abroad for some sunshine. But if you really want to keep it, I've got some money in the bank to give you for your eighteenth. I've been saving for years. You can use it for driving lessons and the test fee. How about that?"

Chad thought and frowned. He knew he could push her aside and do what he liked. However, the kindness of her pleading did brush his hidden heart and she was offering him a good deal. This way he could be legal, unlike his old man, and still have a lot of fun in the process.

She knew he was considering her proposal. "For me, Chad," she said in her softest voice.

He was struck by a recollection, one shadow filled night years ago when he had heard her sobbing and gone to the door of her bedroom with every intention of going inside. He imagined himself putting his face into her neck and weeping too, holding tight until she thanked him and their shared their moist cheeks in an embrace. She must have needed something like that, the kind of hug his father never gave. Chad had turned away then because he thought it was weak to show emotion. When he realised his father always did the same he had ended up hating himself for being so cold. He owed her a little compassion.

"Okay. But I get the money right away. I want my first lesson tomorrow."

"We'll go to the bank now," Val agreed.

He dropped her to one side strode out onto the pavement with a swagger, like a gunslinger ready to draw. While Val clung to the doorframe he viewed his prize with hungry eyes. A beautiful, sleek length of fluorescent blue that stood against the grey of the street and whispered a promise of wilder and grander things over distant horizons.

"I gonna burn the rubber off those tyres," he said, with a grin.

CHAPTER FIVE

Chad passed his driving licence at the first time of asking. Val had predicted this outcome, with feelings mixed between wishing him well and severe dread of the consequences. He had applied himself to the task with frightening determination, listening intently to the instructor and studying his Highway Code constantly in the way he used to do his homework.

"Now the fun starts," he declared that afternoon when he burst into the laundrette to share the triumph with his mother.

She was emptying one of the machines with some damp brown socks in her hand dripping water onto the floor.

She sighed. "You will be careful, won't you?"

"We've been over this."

"Chad, I'm your mother. I don't have a choice."

"Don't worry!" he replied.

They both knew he was going to be anything but careful. The words just had to be exchanged like a ritual that satisfied their instincts as parent and son. And she would worry. That was obvious.

"Thanks, mum," he remembered to say, before disappearing out to the car and the world full of new possibilities it provided.

~

Val could hear him drive into their street long before Chad clattered up their steps and in through the door. She shuddered not because of the noise but in fear of the day she didn't hear it, the day he didn't return, the despondent silence that would follow after he had killed himself at the wheel.

She stood at the kitchen door and watched him strut past in his tight white t-shirt and tighter jeans. He'd got partly up the stairs when she could keep calm no longer.

"You don't give a damn do you?" she said.

He stopped, appearing to wait for more.

"I asked you to be careful in that car. I could hear you from in here. You're heading for a smash and I'll be left to pick up the pieces."

He turned to look down on her. He wore that same challenging expression he always had now, like he was expecting a fight with everyone he encountered. "It's the way I am," he shrugged.

"No," she countered, advancing on him. "You were always a sweet boy. I know there's a heart within."

"You raised me, sure," he agreed. "So whatever I am now is down to you."

"This is your dad speaking," she said.

He winced at the mention of him. She reached up and laid a pale hand on the bare muscle of his arm.

"Don't risk everything just to be cool," she pleaded.

He contemplated her and saw all that was small, frail and sad. The effect she could have on him was irritating.

"What am I risking? I've got nothing! So I go out in that motor and let the engine unwind. When I'm at speed I feel strong and free. I can go anywhere and be anyone. I meet others like me and we race."

Val cried out loud and sank onto the bottom stair. Chad came closer, crouching down to dish out yet more.

"Oh yes, we race. No one wears a seatbelt. We love the thrill of it, the danger, the not knowing if something big might happen at any time. It's a bug that's in my blood now. The only place to be, where I'm alive. Not in this shit neighbourhood with a washed up mother who got left behind."

Val stayed put long after he'd slammed himself inside his room. His view of her was cruel but not wrong. All she'd managed was to bring him up and judging by his attitude she could add that to her list of failures. What was there to do? She got up and made dinner.

~

He came and sat at the table when she called him. "Sorry, mum," he said.

He took her silence as an acceptance. "I get such stuff in my head. I think I drive in hope of leaving it all behind."

"Well you can't," she declared, dropping a plateful in front of him.

"I don't want to get stuck in this crummy life."

She settled in opposite and gestured for him to eat. "Well, it was you who messed up your exams. But you were always bright and the few passes you got can still help you get a better job than at the chip shop."

"I'm not listening," he said, concentrating on his food in hope she would leave him alone.

"I could do with some more money coming in," she continued. "I have two mouths to feed."

"Well, I'll leave then," he retorted, with a smug smile.

He knew she'd hate for him to go and so wouldn't push him any further.

They carried on without further exchange until he got up to go.

"You realise he'll be back for the car just as soon as he can," she said.

"It's mine, whether he tries to reclaim it. I'll stand in his way."

Val cringed at the thought of the confrontation and clutched her jaw to stifle a whimper.

"Look. It's like I said before. I love the speed, the guys I hang out with. I'm only doing what I need to. You're good to me mum, I admit that. I just have to follow my sense. You nag, I escape. One day I'm gonna keep on driving, right away, and find fortune on the road."

Val cracked. "Oh, you sound just like your father!" she screamed.

Chad was flummoxed. He didn't want to hear her say this. In search of a worthy response, he looked around the tiny kitchen and found only a howling woman in drab clothes. He picked up a fork from the table and threw it at the wall. When it clattered to the floor all was quiet. He turned and left.

~

Greg Jackson was found dead in Birmingham during the latter part of January 1977. There had been much snow and the body was revealed by the thaw, his hand the first to appear, sticking up through the ice, the red birthmark turned black by the ice in his veins. It was concluded that he froze to death following an assault that broke both his legs. No clue was ever found to who had carried out the attack.

When the news reached Val in London she was at home alone. She sat in the tiny lounge for over two hours, the walls close and her meaninglessness summed up by a total lack of feeling. She was heavy like the dust on the coffee table. The ashes of unfulfilled life.

"I must get out of here," she concluded, and went to the minimarket.

On her way she passed the Jensen, parked in seeming innocence nearby. The front grill grinned malevolently as if it knew the power it bestowed on whoever sat at its wheel. For Val, it represented the stupid folly of an idiot living a lie. And a danger to her son.

She shopped idly, without the usual attention to prices or hunt for bargains. Everyone was going about their mundane business, unaware she was just a shell, no more alive than the cardboard cut out of a man standing at the vegetable stall, grinning with his armfuls of produce. If anyone real did smile at her, she would never have noticed.

She stopped by the car again on the walk home and put a foot up on the back bumper. She wanted to push it away, make it be gone before it turned Chad into Greg. But all her force was never going to have any effect. She got back as Chad returned from his lunchtime shift at the chip shop. Only now did Greg's death seem tragic.

They met at the steps up to the front door. He hardly acknowledged her even though she'd seen nothing of him the previous evening, and he made no offer to relieve her of the heavy shopping bags of burden. She waited while he put his key in the lock.

"Chad, your father is dead," she said.

He turned to look at her. She watched the last vestiges of childhood steal from his face. He spoke no words. There was a sense of resolution in his

37

walk away down the hall and his immediate reappearance with the car keys spinning on his finger.

~

"Chad used to draw funny faces and wear them as masks to cheer me up." Maria released a smile, wide and white, and her impossibly dark eyes sparkled. With her mass of black hair, chaotic yet perfect, and skin of silk, she was beautiful. Sat beside Chad, his strong protective arm around her, she wriggled deliciously as she laughed.

"Mum, do you have to keep dragging up my childhood," Chad complained.

"Maria asked me what you were like," Val explained.

"Yes, it is okay," Maria said. "I get so little from him. I want to know."

Maria's voice had a slight accent to it, lending a mystery to her aura. She threw Chad a playful glance full of long lashes.

Val continued. "He collected the plastic models you get in the cereal packets and he'd play out little stories with them to me on the kitchen table. He even made scenery out of cardboard to make them more realistic."

"Oh, that's wonderful!" Maria exclaimed.

Chad was less impressed and scowled, his jaw stony. "They were crap," he said.

Maria ignored his pain and wanted more. "What were they about, these–"

"Stop now!" Chad shouted.

"Chad!" his mother protested. "Don't get so angry."

"Enough piss taking," he insisted.

An uncertain silence fell on the little lounge. Maria spoke first to break the deadlock.

"Can I use the bathroom?"

When Chad did not offer a response, Val directed her, giving Chad a sharp stare in the process. They both watched Maria's bottom twitch out of the room for different reasons.

"Oh, my goodness," Val said, holding her hand to her neck. "She's totally divine."

"Yeah, she sure is," Chad agreed, his mind clearly recalling an intimate moment with her.

"And she deserves better behaviour from you."

Chad sat up in his defence. "No, it's your fault. Why do you need to embarrass me? It's enough having to bring her to this dive."

"Oh, I'm sorry if this is not good enough. I suppose she comes from the suburbs?"

"What's wrong with that? It's my bad luck to have losers for parents."

"Stop it! We can do better than this. Let's show our manners."

He didn't voice his agreement but remorse was clear on his face.

"Well, I thought she'd be such a silly, vacant girl when you told me you'd met hanging around the industrial estate. And yet she's the real deal."

"You get the real deal when you have wheels," Chad boasted.

Maria came back in wearing a frown and did not return to her seat. "I heard you arguing. Is everything all right?"

Chad and Val exchanged a look of uncertainty.

"We were talking about your trips out in the car," Val ventured. "I was wondering what possesses you to stand in a car park in the winter."

"Oh, it's cool," Maria declared, relaxing and joining Chad again on the sofa. "Or kind of. You get to hook up with the best people." She patted Chad's outstretched leg.

"You wouldn't understand, mother. Us young need to get away. Out there we can express ourselves, compare cars and drive the circuit."

"The circuit?"

When Chad tutted in disbelief at his mum's ignorance, Maria scowled at him. She drew a breath that lifted her torso up and emphasised her curves all the more. Thus she combined beauty with authority as she explained what he meant.

39

"It is a set route. You all do it. Sometimes fast, sometimes slowly. The engines rumble, the music's loud. We let the world know we're there."

"Sounds awful."

"I think of it as a way that our generation can find a voice. We have meaning together."

She spoke lucidly and with great belief. Val was envious and needed to throw back a negative. "Cold, dark, wet, empty. That's what it sounds like to me."

Chad sat forward. "It would to you. I've got some real mates. Top mates."

"And I bet there's alcohol and drugs."

"Cigarettes. That's all I use," Maria said.

Chad shook his head. "There's some stuff kicking about. Most want a clear head to drive their motors."

"And you?"

Val was probing for answers. Maria saw this and avoided more confrontation.

"Chad has the best car of all. He is king of the strip."

"So it follows that you are his queen," Val reasoned.

Maria blushed but remained stoic. "I know a good heart and Chad has the biggest. I'm with him for that, nothing else."

"Devotion comes at a price," she told her. "A price you have to be sure you can pay."

~

Val waited up until she heard the growl of the Jensen returning. He was surprised to find her hunched at the kitchen table in her dressing gown, balancing a cup of cocoa on her knees. He actually joined her for a change, his sharp blue eyes watchful. She guessed the reason he'd elected to sit with her tonight rather than crash in his room was Maria. He wanted to know what she thought of her.

"So what can I hear in Maria's voice. Something foreign?"

40

"Spanish," Chad answered quickly. "Her dad is Spanish."

"I thought it was."

Chad waited for his mum to expand on her observations. She sipped her drink, relaxed and thoughtful, but remained quiet. Chad tapped the keys on the table, impatiently. She smiled inside, pleased to see he cared.

"So what do you think of her?" he demanded.

"Maria?"

"Of course, Maria."

Val tried to sound as casual as possible. "Yeah, she's okay." She couldn't look at him for fear of laughing. From the corner of her eye she was aware he was incensed.

"You don't get it all," he snapped and thumped his fist on the table.

"Don't be silly, Chad. I was joking. She's fabulous, like the sky on a sunny day."

He relaxed now and lay back in the chair, gazing into the ceiling as if that big blue firmament was visible right there.

"With her I feel so fulfilled. I can't explain it properly. Reaching the top of the mountain, I suppose. You know you used to tell me how you wished you could swim with dolphins, well, I'm doing just that being with her."

She saw him in this moment, released from the darkness of disappointment, and had to let him drift away on the cloud when all of her instincts told her to pull him back to the safety of her bosom. Her little boy was entering a realm in which she could not defend him.

She had deep envy for Maria's looks and obvious determination. That free spirit that danced through her slim limbs and tight flesh was the direct opposite to Val's downtrodden acceptance of hopelessness. Maria flew while Val trudged. She danced on a higher plain than Chad had ever seen and Val worried about the future. If Maria ever dropped him back down to the shit on the ground, he might never emerge again.

41

The alternative was the two of them finding happiness. Val would be left behind, lost without the only thing she lived for. This was a crossroads every mother reached, except in her case all directions led to dead ends. All this she kept to herself.

Chad stretched and yawned, exhausted from his expressions of love.

"I need sleep," he admitted.

"Thank you for letting me meet her," Val said.

"You're kidding. She's been nagging me about coming here to see you."

"Oh," Val squeaked and a little chuckle squeezed out. "Well, there's even more reason to take care now isn't there?"

Chad smiled at her calculated logic. "Good night, mother." He bent over and kissed her cheek, something he hadn't done in a long time. "And I'm sorry for you about dad."

She didn't cry until he had gone up the stairs. They were quiet, gentle tears. And she spoke only once she was sure he would not hear.

"He only ever did two things of any importance, and both happened in a back alley. One was making you and the other was dying."

~

"Hey Chad, howya doing big guy?"

"I'm good."

The two boys clenched the others upturned hand and made a united fist. Chad and his main sidekick, Jonny, did this every time they met. Each had the same style clothes, designer jeans and a tight t-shirt, boots and leather jacket. Both wore their hair long and their face mean. They parked their cars and girlfriends casually, left the door open wide and the music up loud. There wasn't much conversation. The odd funny quip and a cigarette were shared while they surveyed their kingdom. The empty car parks and service roads of offices and warehouses were slick with rain and glowed under the lonely glow of streetlamps. Docklands that had once attended to an empire lay barren and forgotten and the youth of the 1970s made it their domain.

42

There were many here. Lots more like Chad and Jonny, spending their nights away from responsibility and conformity. Except Chad was exceptional. He had a motor that was a genuine racer and not some patchwork Ford souped-up for effect.

Maria got herself out of the car and found the other girlfriends hanging out on a wall above the river. They made the fashion statements that teenagers found essential to give them some identity. Hats and shirts, flowing skirts, knee length boots and voluminous hair. In this, Maria led the way too.

When the moment was right, Chad gave a signal and they all made ready to leave. The golden couple went first and the cavalcade followed. They took to the circuit. From there it was a free for all. Those who didn't break down or get stopped by police would meet up back at the start or somewhere outside the city. There might be food, drink or drugs shared round and later, relaxed and influenced by whatever they had consumed some would steal away for uncomfortable sex in back seats.

Chad gripped the gear stick and rammed it hard into top. The rev counter spiked and the engine responded in front of them, under that long hood of glossy metal. It was an all conquering statement of power, a release from the shackles. Maria grinned as she was pushed deep into her seat as the roar from the tyres grew louder. They had the sun roof open, despite the cold draft, and their music sang out from the dashboard as a statement to the world beyond. The queue at the cinema, the security guard at the power plant, the jet plane in the black sky above, the empty school, all were humbled by this dream in silvery blue.

This particular night led them to a hillside overlooking leafy Surrey. That swathe a green belt designed to keep London in check became a temporary haven for those trapped within. The group spread out on the grass under a dome of incredible stars. Blankets were laid down and tins of beer burst open. There were some laughs as a few recounted their feats of great skill on their journey. Everyone got cold very quickly and couples retreated to their cars. Maria liked it best when they did this because she got Chad to herself.

She sat up on her knees, feeling the soft leather on her legs, leaning an elbow on the dashboard and picking at the remains of a bag of chips. Chad assumed his usual pose in driver's mode, laid back with one strong hand stretched out to the steering wheel.

"Your mother is very sweet, and brave," she said.

"She's small minded and easily dominated," Chad countered.

Maria looked stunned. Chad would not meet her eye.

"She let my father treat her like shit. She let her parents treat her like shit. She lets me treat her like shit. How can that be brave?"

"To keep going through all that," she replied. "Holding her life together."

"I call it stupid. I don't want to end up like her."

"What else can she do?"

"She didn't have to let it slip away. She's taken the easy path. Do nothing and cling to what you have."

Maria drew in a deep breath. "She loves you," she pointed out.

Chad's body tightened. "I'd rather she stopped worrying about me and got out there before she's too old. She's as good as dead now."

Maria reached out a laid a soft palm on his shoulder. "You see, you do care."

Chad maintained his hardened frame and tapped his fingers on the wheel. It was time to fly.

"Tell me about your dad?" Maria asked.

"Why?"

"I'm curious."

Chad's scowl was visible even in the pale moonlight. "I don't want to speak about him. He gave me nothing."

She stretched her hands out wide. "What about this car?"

44

Chad turned to her now. "I would rather have had time with him. To have walked as a two to school, go out to the cinema together, share an ice cream on Southend pier."

"Of course," she said, wanting to reach for him.

"So don't mention him again. I wished he would go away and that one's been granted."

"Chad," Maria breathed, and squeezed his arm.

He glanced down at her hand. Her delicate fingers were firm but soft as they pressed against the rising veins of his bicep. He raised his eyes back up at her, and started the engine.

"Let's go someplace secluded," he declared, and tore off down the road with real purpose.

~

Shortly afterwards, in a dark lay-by under the Jensen's curved roof, Maria lay back and let Chad unleash his manhood. It was over quickly and without words. He climbed across to the driver's seat as Maria recovered her lace panties from the foot well.

Once she had restored her dignity she sat up on the wide arm rest and leaned herself against his shoulder. His breath was still short from his exertion.

"You know, you could go a little slower. Maybe, we could try and enjoy each other a bit more."

"Wasn't it good?" he asked.

"Oh, it was. I just wish you'd take your time," she purred. "Let me show what I can do for you."

He thought about this for a while, her delicate nose caressing his neck.

"Sex is no big deal," he sniffed.

"It can be," she sighed, brushing her palm across his chest, feeling the dampness of his sweat.

45

"I used to hear my dad fucking my mum. He'd stay away for ages and she'd be pissed off with him, and yet after a few hours and some fancy gifts, they'd do it. I hated him for taking her like that, and mum for allowing him. I couldn't look at them at breakfast.

"So I decided the whole thing must mean nothing. Mum took him inside her when I knew she felt nothing but contempt."

"She must have had love for him, too."

"You're joking! It wasn't like your happy little homestead."

"They made you, that is fantastic."

"Oh yeah, in and out in a flash," Chad snarled.

Maria pouted. "The same as you just did with me."

Chad shrugged and Maria sat back. She waited in vain for him to make a connection. Instead, he twiddled a few knobs on the dashboard and shuffled his booted feet.

"So why not be better than them?" she pleaded, gripping his arm with both hands.

"Because I can't be."

"Really?"

He moved uncomfortably, turning away, shaking her off and looking out the side window. Maria was perplexed. She thought her magic was strong enough to bridge the chasm between his pain and her hope. With a groan, she got out and went and leaned on the front of the car with her back to Chad. He fidgeted for a while, glancing at her unmoving silhouette under the moon that had just cleared the horizon, until he couldn't stand it any longer.

"It's beautiful," he said, coming up alongside and slipping his arms around her waist.

She dropped her mass of hair against his chin and her eyes reflected the earth's satellite that smiled down on them. "Stunning. So bold in a sea of blackness. It always looks so strong."

46

"I can be better," he whispered.

"Do you think?"

"I need time."

She turned and then moved her head back to get his face in focus. "I can give you that, sure. If you make some effort, get this anger out of your head. Maybe come to yoga class with me. That can teach you to relax. It gives you lots of space to think and work out where you fit.

"Just don't expect me to be anything like the way you see your mum. I'm not a plank to walk across when the ground gets a bit soggy. I have big dreams and places to reach far beyond this scene here. I want to share them with someone with the same desire as me. The human experience is to be savoured. Join me, Chad. My personal journey is heading for something life changing."

CHAPTER SIX

When Maria Arizmendi climbed into Chad's Jensen for the final time, she very nearly got straight back out. He refused to venture inside and meet her parents, despite a firm promise when he'd dropped her off a few nights before.

"But why not?" she demanded. "I got to know your mum months ago."

"It'll be too nice in there. Your house looks beautiful, full of stuff I never saw. And they'll be everything I'd have wanted. I'll end up feeling shitty."

"And what about how they're feeling? Or me?

"They'll stop you seeing me once they know I'm not like them."

Maria's pretty face was outraged. "No! They're more likely to mistrust you if you stay away."

"Oh, please."

Chad retreated into his sanctuary of silence. She waited, to see if her luscious lashes blinking over big brown eyes might stir a positive reaction. This was a critical moment in their relationship, one to test their ability to reach across the intangible line of class. Each was breathing solidly, sending a mist across the windscreen. Beyond, the blackening sky sent down great drops of water that clattered onto the bonnet. Maria lost patience.

"Come on, I'll be there with you. They are judgemental people. I have their trust. It's a natural interest they have."

"I'll think about it. Your mine right now, that's all I care about."

At this moment she put her hand on the shiny door handle and prepared to leave. This was a splendid car. She was unable to think the same about the owner. Her principles were strong. If she walked away from him now it would be final. As she gave Chad one last chance to say the right thing, the rain got much heavier, pounding loudly on the roof and windscreen.

"Let's get out of here," Chad said, and swung his mighty car around heading for the river.

"You can't run away from everything, you know."

"Maybe I can."

They each retreated into silence, with a similar expression of unhappiness, yet neither was prepared to help the other. When they drew up in the car park with a mighty skid all the assembled followers turned to see them. When no one emerged, Jonny strolled over. Chad buzzed the window down.

"You okay, man?"

Chad kept his hands on the wheel and his eyes ahead. Jonny was hunched against the rain that blew in a stiff breeze off the water. He could see Maria was equally quiet.

"You two had a little disagreement?"

Maria threw him a harsh glance. Chad rolled his jaw around and looked up at the blackened buildings ahead.

"Kind of," he admitted.

"You were smiling a whole lot more with Patty last night."

"Patty?" Maria repeated, her voice registering high.

Chad scowled at his supposed pal who was wearing an idiotic grin. "You're such a knob, Jonny."

Chad took off, spinning the wheel aggressively through his hands and speeding away. Maria felt the chilling realisation of what a lottery love could be. Even she, with all the charms, could be made to look a fool. She was full of irritation.

"Stop the car," she ordered.

Chad sighed and pulled up opposite a greasy cafe. They had shared a frothy hot chocolate behind that steamy window, no more than six weeks ago, kissing the cream off the other's lips and laughing at the mess they made. How quickly the joy had dissolved. Now her tender frame was hard and arched while he looked down somewhere between his feet, unable to meet her eye.

"Patty," she said, simply.

Chad shrugged. "It was nothing. We just drove round."

"She's with Dan."

"Not any more. They split last week."

Maria took a moment to assess this new information. "So you took her out as a mercy mission?"

"She was on her own," Chad explained.

"Oh, that's okay then," she said, ironically.

"Look. You've been too busy."

"Two nights!"

"Well."

"My aunt came to stay. I've not seen her for six months."

"Big deal."

She looked at him, for the first time since they had stopped. He had no understanding of family bonds.

"You could have been there too if you had the courage to meet my family."

"I can....."

"What?"

Chad was defeated. Maria was too clever and open and lovely for him to ever keep up with.

Maria, on the contrary, was not finished. "So, why Patty? If it was just a drive, why get involved?"

"I take what I can get," Chad said.

"Well, I don't!" Maria exclaimed.

Now Chad turned to face his antagonist. "Oh, come on. Everybody's been around a bit, just to kill time."

"Not me, Chad," Maria said, her tone definite as she directed her entire essence at him. "Not me."

"We can't all be perfect," he said.

Maria sighed. "This evening just keeps getting worse."

Chad's mask was slipping. He wanted to break down in front of her, show himself as the coward he really was. She was so charismatic, even with her eyes closed to the pain of the situation, a sweet peach growing in a concrete jungle. For once, that exquisiteness might be spared its fateful destruction. He could be a protector. Instead, he fell back into the part his father always played.

 "We'll go back to the crowd. We can go cruising. Show 'em we're cool."

"Actually," Maria announced. "Let's not."

"What then?"

She had grown up with a doctrine of success. If you took something on and it got difficult, you tried harder, looked for the way to a solution. She didn't want to admit defeat in her first serious relationship.

"Just drive for a bit," she said. "Anywhere. Maybe we can clear our heads."

"Okay."

Chad figured he owed her that and let the car run. They weaved through the traffic. He turned the music on loud and showed off his skill with the gears and the power of the engine as they beat everyone when the lights went green.

He took them into smarter parts of the city, Kensington and Chelsea, where the houses were big and the wide windows revealed splendid interiors with fine art walls and grand fireplaces. Maria began to enjoy the ride.

Ahead a large puddle had formed in the gutter and beside it on the pavement a smart old lady was walking slowly with her back to them.

"Let's give her a fright!" Chad said.

"No!" Maria begged.

He ignored her. The wide wheels of the Jensen roared as they created a perfect arc of water that swamped her fur coat and hat and made her stagger.

51

"Bingo!" he shouted, watching her in his mirror and cackling.

"That was clever?!" Maria protested.

"Rich cow, she had it coming to her."

Maria was tearing up inside. She adored Chad and hated him. Love was never supposed to be this confusing. He had a desperate, broken heart and despite all her efforts to heal him, he was still an asshole. It was her turn to seek a place to hide.

"Take me home," she hissed. "Now."

"Oh, come on," Chad retorted. "It was just a bit of fun."

"You don't know what fun is."

"Right, best you go home then. You can be sure to get some fun there."

Now Chad put all his focus into driving as rapidly as was practically possible. The street lights flashed on the windscreen as they went ever faster. He reached for her hand and found it wedged hard between her legs beyond his grasp.

His father's face appeared before him. Chad had tried so hard to not be like him, to revolt against the loathsome way he treated people and his disregard for morals. But Chad was what life had made him. He slipped into a pattern and his dreams went with them.

He hit the steering wheel with his fist. This car hadn't helped at all. It represented what Greg had been; flashy, noisy, overblown, and false. He regretted ever craving it for himself. Now he wanted the chance to search for clemency in Maria. If only he could get the words out.

What a child was doing out on a bike so late was not an important question after he had appeared so suddenly at the end of the Jensen's bonnet. Chad was deep in a reverie, imagining the joy in Maria's forgiveness. His young reactions were sharp. By some miracle he avoided the boy, swinging the car away, up on to the pavement and back down, screaming onto the brake until the near side hit a concrete based litter bin.

Maria, who had twisted round to check no one had been hit, was thrown forward so hard she left a permanent dent in the dashboard. The back of her head took the full force of the impact and in an instant life was changed for so many people.

CHAPTER SEVEN

Chad finally met Maria's parents. It was in the cold courtroom where his conviction was pronounced, his driving licence was lost and the fine was imposed. Their expressions were grim, laced with desperately deep sorrow. The delights which could have followed if he'd gone in and seen them that night, instead of driving off to his doom, would never be realised.

Mr Arizmendi stared at Chad for the entire hearing, like a snake fixed on its prey, ready to strike. Mrs Arizmendi sobbed audibly, gasping with a desperation that cut through Chad's frozen heart. There was no sign of Maria. Chad directed his attention downwards. Val looked up, to the high ceiling where the lights buzzed behind yellowing plastic.

Chad's plunge to total misery was complete. All he had cherished was gone. The car now an emblem of his stupidity. His former friends a reminder of a pointless way of living. Only his mother stood by him

"You're not alone," she whispered, laying a hand on his.

He pulled away. Her loyalty was, once again, pathetic, her love meaningless. This was the same woman who had been devoted to his father.

Maria's father was kept a distance away. It was clear he wanted to invoke his own version of justice on the stupid kid who hadn't even had the decency to dress smartly for the hearing. Chad might have welcomed a deadly blow. His life had no significance any more.

"I hope you're happy you destroyed us!" Maria's dad shouted as they were escorted from the room.

In a tiny chamber at the back, Chad tried to see beyond the bland floor. His mind held a picture of Maria's face, beautiful in her nakedness as they made love. They were at a fantastic beach he invented in his dreams, where the sand dunes swept up high and hid them from a harsh world. The full moon

54

shone off the big bonnet of the Jensen. Everything fell into place. They knew they had found the well of happiness.

"She was the one for me," he stated.

Val didn't know how to reply. He had spat all her words back at her since the accident. So she sat motionless by his side, in hope that a day would come when he could smile again.

~

The dreaded car stared back at Val from the road, with a front grill grinning despite the hell wrought upon their life. Chad would not, could not, have anything to do with it. So she had decided to sell the thing to a dealer at whatever price she got offered. The money was irrelevant. She just wanted every trace of that overblown monster gone.

She was sitting outside. The place could be so hot in the summer and the walls were always closing in again. From the doorstep she would see Chad coming home all the sooner. He'd been gone three days now.

She glanced out periodically towards the turning that led to the Underground. It was like this with Greg in the early years. The number of books and magazines she'd read during the long hours of waiting would stretch to across London and back.

Today she received an unexpected visitor. She didn't see her at first. A young girl in a wheelchair was easily hidden beneath the walls and hedges that the folks used around here to give them some separation from the blandness beyond. When she appeared at the gate, Val took in an involuntary lungful of air and grimaced.

"Maria? What a surprise!" she gasped, unsure how to act.

"I'm here to speak to Chad," Maria said.

"He's not here. He's gone away."

"Run away?"

"He's coming back," Val asserted. "I think."

The two advanced on one another.

"You look–"

"Different," Maria interrupted. "I'm a fucking cripple, that's why."

Val held her hands up to her cheeks. "I was going to say well. You look well."

"Considering."

Val crouched down to meet her eye to eye. Maria's were still dark and deep, more determined than ever. Her own remained washed out, watery and restless. She swayed, overwhelmed by the sight of such a beautiful form trapped in an ugly metal contraption.

"Sorry, I'm just a bit shocked to see you."

"Because I'm the enemy."

"I don't blame you."

"It was my statement that condemned him. I told the police he was driving like an idiot."

"I know," Val said, softly, her shoulders sagging. "And he knows. He's lost without you. He sleeps through the days, goes out in the night. I can't talk to him anymore."

"So he'll have wanted to see me today?"

Val's face brightened and lifted. "Oh yes!"

"I think not. I would have been horrible to him."

"So that's why you've come? To inflict more pain?"

Maria gripped her chair until her knuckles went white and wheeled it up close to Val, who turned her head away. Maria leaned forward, her black locks tumbling, and brought her mouth near to Val's ear.

"I've decided not to push for a settlement. My old life, the prospects I and my parents worked hard to create, have been destroyed by your useless shit of a son. My despair is his one achievement, probably his only achievement. I know he could never pay any sum to me as compensation, no more than you might for him. Your existence is as sorry as his."

56

Maria's words stabbed at Val's shrivelled heart, inflicting more wounds when it seemed impossible for it ever to bleed again.

"Now look at me."

Val slowly complied, but only partially. She felt threatened and she shook as she viewed her assailant sidelong.

"See how I have changed. Trapped in this chair, I am affected for life. I can't hide out, paint a brave face, bury the fear. All of me is on display, broken. Half a person. He might try to forget me but his work is part of me, without end."

"I'm so sorry, Maria," Val sniffed.

"Don't be. You have your own punishment to bear and sitting out here on this step won't lead to an escape. You too can never be free of this. Because you've lost all your chances with him. And that is enough for me, knowing how much you will suffer for that, raising a son to be as bad as his father.

"And Chad has thrown away me and my love. I intend to be an achiever, a power of inspiration and spirit. My future is bright, I am determined to succeed. I leave him behind in his torture. He will be without sight, feeling, hope, unable to move on. There is no one after me. In this way I kill him."

Val watched her wheel away with surprising speed, never once looking back, content with the message she had delivered. A breeze blew up from nowhere, producing impossible goose bumps for a hot July afternoon on Val's pale arms, onto which dropped her tainted tears.

~

Maria's predictions proved to be very intuitive. Val read about her in the newspaper, campaigning for rights for the disabled and having her picture taken with a famous actor who became her husband.

Val never saw Chad with another girl. The boy was a shattered shadow about the place. She had managed to keep him near her but what a price

57

they'd paid. And she never actually had him with her again. He was beyond reach, always cold, and the emptiness in his eyes never changed.

She would lie awake at night worrying. He came and went but what might happen if he left permanently? Ultimately, she knew it made no difference. Either way she had nothing.

CHAPTER EIGHT

"Hold on tight for a fast ride!" Carol proclaimed as she steered the big Jensen out of the parking lot and onto the road.

The mounting excitement was mingled with terror. Everyone else seemed to be going about their business without a second thought. Cars flashed by, pedestrians stepped into the traffic, dodging and skipping, cyclists plodded with determination through narrow gaps in the mayhem and toddlers teetered on the curb side, ready to dive beneath her wheels.

A horn blasted when she pulled out of a junction. She had failed to appreciate how fast an oncoming van was travelling. As she jerked to a stop and stalled, she was left looking up at the unsympathetic face of a very beefy man. He threw his hands up and shook his chubby head at her. "Stupid fucking cow!" were the words she was sure she could read on his slobbering lips.

She mouthed a sorry back and held up a palm. This appeased him for a moment until he glanced into his mirror and indicated she should get a move on, right now. It was Val's turn to curse as she failed repeatedly to get started again. Her legs flapped uselessly as she tried to get her feet set firmly on the pedals. By the time she did manage to pull away, her judge had crossed his flabby arms and dropped his head to one side in complete contempt.

In anger, she switched off the distracting music. As she fretted forwards, Marcus came into her mind. Why did she always refer back to him? She didn't want to have any thoughts of him. The urge to get away grew stronger.

~

"Good god, Marcus, do you really think that little of me? To do such a thing!"

59

His reaction was unruffled as usual. He stood calmly across the other side of the lounge they had decorated together as newlyweds, his hands in pockets, perfectly manicured and unflustered. He never lost that assured air. Those damned good looks, chiselled cheek bones and temples, might have aged but remained as alluring as the rising full moon in a cobalt sky.

"We've reached that point," he said, as if his decision on the matter was final.

She knew he was right. But how could he be so cold about the whole thing? Fourteen years together coming to an end. She wasn't one of his business transactions.

"Maybe you could have talked to me, before shagging someone else?" she suggested.

"It makes no difference, the order of such things. The result is the same."

"And my feelings?"

He moved his perfect jaw from side to side as if he was tasting some ice cream. "Painful either way," he concluded.

He was so decided about everything! Even in this. She fell back into the sofa and tried to find an answer in the swirl of the rug.

"You don't want to work at our marriage?" she asked, already knowing his answer.

"It would be futile. I need to move on. Fiona is—"

"Don't say her name in front of me!" Val snapped.

Marcus appeared put out by her demand. "She's a breath of new life, a spring."

"Younger and a better fuck," Val countered.

"Oh please!" he complained. "There's more to it than that I assure you."

"And what of me?"

He assessed her part in this magical equation of his. "Well, it's a chance for you too. A new start. You've always told me I've suffocated you. Go and live a little."

60

"Thanks," she said, almost feeling she should be grateful. "What about Richie?"

"He's eleven," he said.

"I know that!"

"He can make his own decisions about where he spends his time. You and I are mature enough to respect him."

He could afford to be smug. Richie loved his father's strength. He was draw to him like a magnet. Mum would have to play second fiddle, fill in when he was busy with work.

"Most of this house is mine," Carol reminded him. "My dad practically bought it for us."

"You'll get your dues. I can borrow against the company. The new deal just got signed, it's going to be a bumper year."

"How nice for you and your new little woman."

Marcus stared at his aging wife as she sat hunched in the chair, clutching her knees in desperation. She would find it hard without his guidance.

"I'll give you as much support as you need," he assured her. "Help you get on your feet."

"I don't want anything from you!" she screamed, and stood up unaided. "I can find a new path without your interference."

She stomped from the room without glancing back to check his reaction.
They had grown apart, it was true but she hated what he had done and how he had gone about it. He was best left behind. And yet, weeks later, alone in her hotel room, she waited for his call.

~

Carol lay on the bed and ate the complimentary biscuits. She used to resist sweet treats to try and hang on to her figure. Now Marcus had found a fresh, curvier option it no longer mattered. At least not until she worked out what to do with the rest of her life.

61

So where to start? It was surprising how little she had once she had decided that their marital home and all the memories were best left behind. Across the room sat two suitcases full of basic clothes, toiletries and paperwork. Back at her mum's house the space dad had used for his model making before he died was now taken up with various bits of her stuff. Some furnishings, crockery and cutlery, shoes, ornaments and photos. There was nothing else. Except for that huge car outside.

She went over to the window and peeked through the curtains. There it was, under the lamp, shining at her, ready to unleash power, in many ways representing what was to come. A challenge to her safe little world. She needed to find the spark within her to match her wheels. That drive back to the hotel had been upsetting.

She called room service and ordered a feast of fried snacks and chips with a double martini. Once it arrived she sprawled out naked on the bed and turned the television onto a fairly steamy drama. All of this was as out of character as buying a car spontaneously.

She rang her friend Lori and updated her on this most amazing of days. "I don't care about the expense right now," she told her.

Lori had always dominated Carol. They'd met at the estate agents, both coming from school. While Carol had plodded through fifteen years without improving her position before being consumed by motherhood, Lori had started her own letting company and now sat pretty at the head of a mini empire.

"The funds will soon run out if you don't make the correct investments," Lori advised. "You'll need me to advise you on the best kind of place."

Carol threw a battered prawn into the air. It ended up nestled between her breasts instead of between her teeth. She laughed in spite of the serious lecture she was receiving.

"Are you all right?" Lori enquired.

"Oh yes," Carol giggled. "Just having fun."

"Well you should at least look to getting straight back on the property ladder. You don't want to end up renting."

"That's rich coming from you!"

"Carol. I do very well out of my tenants. But it is a mug's game. I make the money and they still have nothing at the end. I don't want you to be like one of them."

Lori had contempt for the people from whom she got her living. She could argue publically that she was doing a service to the community, housing those without means to buy, yet Carol knew the real truth. It was profit or profit and nothing else mattered.

Carol was heading in a different direction. "I'm going to climb into that big old car and drive."

"To where?"

"Who knows? Coventry? Amsterdam? California?"

"Don't be daft. What about your job?"

"I quit."

"Tell me that isn't true."

"Sorry, cant. It is true."

Lori was quiet for a moment. Carol enjoyed this rarity while she scrunched up her napkin and threw it with aplomb across the room and into the bin. Having collected her thoughts, Queen Lori passed judgment. "Carol, you are a fool. You're going to need an income. It is important to be steady after the shakeup you've had. And your son deserves stability. Do what you are good at."

"You're so convinced I'm too boring. The time has come to let the dog out of the cage. I can do anything."

"You've been drinking, I can tell. You've talked this rubbish before."

"I mean it now."

"Carol, you are what you are. I'll say it again. You have a son and a liking for normality. You can't become some rootless explorer."

"The bits of that life are sold or getting left behind. That old way didn't work, did it? I'm sick of worrying if Marcus is happy, whether Richie has what he needs for school in the morning. My head is heavy with all of that. I am...." She waved her arms around furiously while she sought the correct word. "Reborn."

"Mad, is what you are."

On the television screen a girl who had been serenaded by a shady character was giving in to passion, ending up pushed face first across a table while receiving his manhood. Carol smirked, turning her head on one side while she imagined the sensations of surrender.

"Looks fun," she said.

"What?"

"You're still there Lori? Sorry, I was distracted."

"It's all one big mistake. When you come running home, you'll have to say to me I was right."

"I won't because I'm not going to be back."

"I'm disappointed in you, Carol. I thought you'd deal with this breakup thing so much better."

Carol took a large swig of martini, feeling a burn in her throat that caught the breath. In the instant after she felt she could leap from the bed and touch the ceiling. Freedom was a blessing!

"You know what I think," Carol said, gripping the phone and staring at a space ahead that she imagined Lori was standing in. "You don't like me becoming this liberated. I'm sitting here, stark naked eating fried junk, dreaming of great sex, thinking about the potential to do anything, with the whole world waiting for me. And you can't deal with it.

"I'm not the dull friend you can look down on and have listen to your latest troubles, any more. I'm going to be tough. Not the lamb you could keep in your flock. Now, I don't know how much I will get wrong. They'll be plenty I

suspect. There's so much to consider. But I'll be doing
something....learning, growing.

"So I'm sorry little Carol has changed, got bigger, big as my new car. And it
is so exciting. Tomorrow I wake up and head on out. Goodbye to you and
don't worry about me. This is the happiest I've ever been."

She put the phone down with a flourish, then thought through her closing
diatribe. That had all come out in a great wave of emotion. Serious stuff.
Did she really mean it?

Half climbing, half falling from the bed she went across to the full length
mirror by the door. This forty two year old body looked okay in the
lamplight. She ran a palm across her tummy. The skin was soft and pulled
pretty nearly flat. Turning to take in the rear view, she wondered if her
buttocks were too plump. She leaned forward and they went tighter. Maybe
once across the table she'd be irresistible to that dark stranger. She closed
her eyes to replay the moment from the television.

Returning to the bed she decided to clear up, take a shower and get some
sleep. If she was going to be true to her word the sun was going to rise on
the first day of her big adventure. At the wheel of her Jensen the
possibilities would be endless.

CHAPTER NINE

"Oh my, what a day!" Carol cried when she opened the curtains.

Outside the light from the sun made all the colours shine so brightly. The sky was already a deep blue. A row of little trees leading to reception had leaves that were an impossibly intense red. Carol smiled at a world that was smiling at her.

"It's made for me."

A man passing by looked in her direction and quickly turned away. Carol frowned, glanced down and saw her nakedness. She disappeared from the window in a fit of embarrassed giggles. But she felt no regrets. She had nothing she wanted to hide.

She bounced through breakfast, eating quickly. She was keen to get going. Her beaming grin was returned by the receptionist as she checked out.

"Going anywhere special today, madam?" she asked, seeing Carol so smart.

"Yes, I am actually. It's a place called new life. I don't quite know where that might be; I just know it will be special."

She left the girl's quizzical expression behind and wheeled her two suitcases over to the car. There was plenty of room in the boot for all her possessions. Before she got in she saw herself in the shining paintwork of the door. She had worn this crimson dress only once, at a business function of Marcus's, and couldn't remember anyone, least of all him, complimenting her choice. So that was then. She was here now, on the edge and ready to jump. She shook Marcus out of her head. Her reflection wriggled and filled it's lungs with fresh air, enjoying the way the thin material clung to the shape beneath.

"Okay, let's do this!" she said, stroking the soft roof of the Jensen like an adulteress caressing her sleeping lover. "You and me. We'll make quite a team."

66

With bare knees and challenging heels she pushed the accelerator hard, determined to remain this positive once she was on the move. At the first set of lights she leaned across, resting her elbow on the smooth wooden central console, and switched on the radio. An unabashed, cheery voice immediately greeted her.

"Welcome to Radio One on this fine morning!"

"A good start!" Carol replied. "Nice to be welcome."

The next bit played out like a movie. She picked her way through the traffic to the rhythm of the music, heading west for no particular reason. The road and adjacent scenery opened out. Her body relaxed, lungs filling with new air. The car began to flow beneath her touch. She was slowly vanishing, ghosting by people and places, none of which would bear any imprint of her passing.

In the rear view mirror, the horizon began to pan out. She felt she was leaving behind much more than just an untidy hotel bed. With each mile, more of her old skin peeled away, taking the decades of dust with it. Beneath she was fresh. Her newly raw senses wanted to touch, smell, hear and see like never before.

The route climbed and soon revealed green wooded valleys and the glimpse of a sparkling river. The urge to stop and go suck in some of the beauty grew strong. At a protracted lay-by she pulled up and clambered out. She leaned on the fence and England's green carpet stretched away as far as she could see, broken only by the occasional hill or sleepy village.

It was a timeless scene. It existed before her and would endure long after she was gone. She was the transitory part. She had to live for this moment and keep on that way. What happened in the future didn't matter. She wanted to feel the same about the past. There was something she had to do.

On the front seat was her bag and on the top, her purse. Inside she found that photo of Marcus and her, taken at a similar height. They had driven up the biggest hill to watch the sunset. Their smiles were wide, arms around each other, her hair blowing in the wind while he remained perfect. She noticed their eyes were looking in different directions. She'd not seen that before. Like they were focused on separate goals. The love had faded from the picture. She used to get it out at work and run her finger across his face. Now she wanted to destroy the stupid thing.

Back at the fence she tore it into a dozen pieces, held her hand aloft and let their tattered memory get carried away by the breeze. She watched the remains float and twist as they drifted down into the woods below.

"Done," she said.

~

The music was coming through strong and fast. She liked the unfamiliar sounds, straying from the safe radio stations of home. With the windows down and sun roof open, she could share the vibe with everyone. An artist she didn't recognise was singing about meaning a lot to someone. Carol wanted to feel like that, make a face light up when she walked in the room. She'd missed that.

When she arrived at a small town it was time to stop for lunch. A building with a large front window surrounded by red paintwork announced itself as the Devil's Kitchen. That sounded good, matching her mood. Parking nearby with surprising ease, she went straight in without her usual pondering and hesitating.

The interior was warm, with a delicious smell of melted cheese and coffee. The exposed brick walls gave it an earthy ambience. She took the best seat with a view of the street. No more seeking the table at the back out of way. She'd had enough of hiding.

There was hardly time to even glance at the menu before a young man approached with a pad and pencil at the ready. He had lovely blue eyes, a cheeky grin and lots of hair that tumbled to his shoulders.

"Hello, madam. What can I do for you?"

68

More than you realise, she thought. "Coffee, for certain," she said, quickly before something stupid came out.

"And a bite to eat?"

She looked at what was on offer. She loved having him focus on her. His attention didn't waver for a moment. That impressed her.

"Oh, I don't know," she breathed. "What do you recommend?"

"The salmon with asparagus is good."

"That's the most expensive meal listed," she countered.

"Treat yourself," he proposed.

"You know," she decided, slapping the menu down. "I think I will."

He smiled and her heart skipped.

"Asparagus is an aphrodisiac," he added.

"Do I look like I need one?"

"I hope so."

She laughed. "Thank you." She peered at his name badge. "Tom. Thank you. You're a fine salesman."

While she waited for the food she got out her compact mirror and assessed herself. Was it the light from the window or did she really seem more luminous today? The grey of her eyes was more solid, confident, with a hint of sparkle. She had a glow of conviction that seemed to smooth out her wrinkles and soften the harder lines. Next she found her lipstick and proceeded to apply it, instantly drawing the attention of fellow diners.

A man at the next table had certainly noticed. He was assessing her in a way that suggested appreciation. When his partner became aware of his diverted interest she chastised him and he apologised. Carol brushed off the contemptuous stare this jealous companion sent her.

"I'm not the one running," she thought.

Tom brought the food over. It smelled delicious and was well presented.

"Wow. Looking good."

"Enjoy," he said, genuinely pleased by her reaction.

69

He returned to place a pink rose into the empty vase on the table. She giggled and he winked. The rest of the world was excluded for the moment. She wasn't the first person in history to strike up sudden strong rapport with someone waiting at their table. For the duration of the meal she luxuriated in her importance to him and let herself dream up fantasies of romance. Food and attention could have this affect. She knew it was just her frame of mind today that allowed her to be carried along by the illusion. What mattered was the sense of freedom.

So it was an added bonus when they were able to share some extra dialogue as she paid the bill. He even sat down opposite. Now she was much closer, she absorbed herself in to his soft hair and elusive long lashes.

"It's my last day here," he told her. "I'm off to polytechnic tomorrow."

"That's cool. Where? Studying what?"

"Stafford. Doing computing."

"Oh." Carol hesitated. "I don't know much about them, except my husband....sorry....ex-husband tells me they are the future."

He rubbed his chin. "I hope so. I got a scholarship."

"You must be bright."

"So I'm told. I hope I live up to expectation."

"You're nervous," she perceived.

"Am I? I guess so." He sat forward. "It's a big step. I'm going to miss my parents, and my little brother."

She liked his honesty and family commitment. It was what she had grown up with. She reached out and squeezed his hand. "You'll be fine. Keep those lovely eyes open to the new ground."

He put up no resistance to her invasion of his space. He, like Carol, emotional on the brink of a big change, had low defences.

"It's going to be hard to leave, but I suppose nothing really has to lose meaning if I approach it on my own terms. What I am inside is the key."

"Oh, that's so true!" she cried.

70

He put his fingers into her palm. "What about you?"

"Me? Well I'm....going somewhere new as well."

"Great. Where?"

"Not sure. I'm kind of making it up."

"Okay. Sounds interesting."

She thought he wasn't convinced by her answer. It needed better explaining.

"I've been part of a marriage, a partnership, until a few days ago when I was ejected. This is all new to me. I'm getting away, looking for a place to start over again. I know it doesn't make much sense. I've just gathered up my bravery and stepped off the cliff."

"Are *you* nervous?" he asked, echoing her question to him.

"You bet. I mean, does anyone really do stuff like this? You see it in the movies but–"

"You're the most fearless person I've ever met," he interrupted. "And yes, you are proof that people do this kind of thing. You're living it now."

Carol suddenly felt as shy as a fourteen year old at her first disco. "Don't be daft," she said.

"I mean it. My leaving home is small fry next to you. I can see it in your eyes. Intensity and carelessness. It's a potent mixture."

Carol laughed. "I've even got the wheels to go with the script. If you look across the road, that blue Jensen is mine."

Tom stood up in the window and took in the vision of super power nestled between a mini and a sorry Leyland product.

"Shit. Now that is cool."

He sat back down and took in all he now saw in Carol. A benchmark on the passage to independence. He refrained from bowing his head, seeing how her chest had flared red with obvious discomfort, matching the bold colour of her dress.

"Time I got back to work. I can see my boss looking at his watch."

71

Carol felt the pain of having to let him go. Her full tummy knotted. "Do you have to?"

"He's a good guy. I don't want to take the piss, I might want to come back at Christmas."

Carol gathered herself, drew in a big breath that raised her breasts, wriggled in her seat, put her elbows on the table and rested her chin on her knuckles. "Take the afternoon off. We can go for a drive. Get to know each other better."

Tom was amazed by her offer. His only girlfriend had dumped him after three weeks and now a mature woman was offering so much after ten minutes of chat.

"I can't. I have to do the right thing here."

Carol had got this far and wouldn't let the chance slip. "Okay, I'll wait until you finish. We can go and drink to the future together."

Now he became properly awkward. "I'm sorry. My folks are picking me up. We are going for dinner, to celebrate my last night. I don't want to let them down."

As he explained this, Carol quietened her pumping heart and suppressed her pulse.

"Of course you can't," she said.

Tom's face betrayed his hurt. Carol didn't want to be the cause of anything like that for him.

"Listen, it was wrong of me to suggest it. We are years apart. My fault. I'm going to go now."

When she stood up he did so too, knocking his chair backwards noisily. Carol glanced around the Devil's Kitchen as it went into a pause. Diners watched the two of them, the owner stopped his drying up and waited for the next part of the act.

"Best of luck," he said. "You're going to be awesome."

He walked up to her, planted a huge kiss on her astonished lips and went off quickly through a door into the kitchen. Carol blinked, gathered her strength, gave everyone a wave and went back to her car.

Once she was out of town she hit a very straight road and let the Jensen go. Its speed was sexy; she felt it in her veins. She had made a pass at a guy young enough to be her son. So what if it hadn't worked out, she was elated with herself for being so bold. She looked in her rear view mirror and saw her smudged lipstick and rosy cheeks. Then a chuckle started that gave way to a long, repeated and resonant laugh fortifying her emancipation. She let it loose and it flew like a wild wind around her. She remembered how prone she used to be to such bouts of hysterical mirth. As a teenager her parents would shake their heads in happy disbelief at her sudden glee. What had suppressed that? Responsibility, the wounds life brings, suppression of thought and word, a lack of excitement. The list might go on endlessly. The fruits of that happy upbringing had been too easily lost.

Time to hit the stop button on all that containment and let her rhapsody free. The true feminine nature of woman was awakening. Her personality had returned, flowering from the dry bones and settled dust of a pallid past. "Watch out world, I'm coming!" she shrieked.

CHAPTER TEN

Carol awoke on the back seat and her legs were cold. Her crimson dress had ridden up and the blanket was in the foot well. She retrieved it, sat up and went into a huddle. The world outside remained dark. She checked that the catch on the door was still down. This was the frontier of her comfort zone, a car park intended for use to visit a bird reserve and not as an overnight stop.

She wondered if anyone was missing her. Marcus certainly wouldn't be. Richie? Perhaps. A picture of him formed. His fresh face with lively eyes so radiant, that perfect skin she would admire while she washed his hair in the bath, the water giving a sheen to his neck and chest. He would chatter away endlessly, carefree, until she lost the thread but remained happy to listen. And best of all, a smile to make you gasp with delight. She remembered some their best days together, an idle walk or a trip to the Science Museum. She realised that wherever she ended up, she had to see her son regularly.

So she was alone in the pitch black, feeling lost. The bravado had been subdued. She'd cut the ties that held her down and after the initial euphoria the sense of drifting was getting unnerving.

"There's not a light in sight," she said, twisting her neck around to take in all sides. "Except....there is."

Grabbing her coat she went out into the gloom and looked up. The fire from a hundred suns burned in the firmament. The longer she stood there, cuddling herself against the chill, the brighter the stars became. She sat on the front bumper of the car and the Universe spoke to her. There was no hiding from space so infinite. A whole load of people on this tiny speck of a planet were restless, worrying about trivialities. Physics wrote this fantastic story on a huge scale and so the fate of all was controlled by that mightiness. She was humbled by the message and moved to gentle tears.

She sighed and lay out across the bonnet. "You're going to show me the way," she called out to the celestial wonder above. "Give me time and I'll read you right."

~

Finding such a clear epiphany of purpose, Carol was happy to drift casually on, parking her beloved car in a fresh place each day. She anticipated oncoming joy like it was her due. Hope carried her along the wet cobbles of a new city, where in the shadow of the cathedral she spent a good hour in a boutique and bought nice clothes. A super long winter coat, a bright scarf, pink lace underwear and stylish boots.

She went to the cinema, the first time she'd ever done that on her own, choosing what she watched rather than having to accommodate someone else's taste. The popcorn was all for her too. It actually wasn't that much of a film. The doing of it mattered more.

She took long drives, the sky changing hue like her thoughts as she imagined new places and sizzling scenarios for herself. She loved being at the wheel, letting the whim of each moment take her along, the vibrations coursing through the chassis and into her very being. She was alive.

Beside a long sandy shore she went slowly, taking in the broad horizon and the helpless seagulls battling against the wind. On the opposite side of the road, an olden wooden fronted building was advertising vacancies for bed and breakfast. She was surprised to find it open in the depths of winter. Despite the flaking white paint and dead plants in pots outside the door, she decided to check in. A proper bed would be welcome after a few nights on the back seat.

The greeting and the room were warm and after a much needed bath in a deep, old style tub, she put on her new things and headed across to the beach. The breeze was keen but she was keener. From toes to finger tips she felt refreshed. The steady, soft crunch underfoot combined with the roar of the receding waves to give her a walking rhythm.

75

She wondered what Marcus would be doing now. Ordering someone around no doubt and chasing the next deal. Life was much more pleasing out here beneath a rocky headland with the hint of salt on the air with no one expecting anything of you.

She moved swiftly on to Richie, submerging herself thoughts of him. This was a more realistic assessment than the one she had used in the car when the darkness had overwhelmed her. She had to admit he had the same shape face as Marcus, only thinner and was prone to red flushes like his mother. His movements were jerky, like he wasn't quite sure of himself yet but didn't want to appear timid. Then there was that irritating habit of chewing his fingers. Such lovely soft hands spoiled by incessant chomping. But he was still only eleven. He was her baby.

She took a rare glance at her watch. Twenty past four. He'd been getting in from school now, eager for tea and biscuits and children's television. Often, he'd sit at the dining room table while she did the ironing and share his thoughts. Marcus would be far too busy at this time of day for the excited ramblings of a schoolboy. She knew she needed to speak to him. She would be able to tell from the tone of his voice whether he was okay.

There had been a phone box by the shop back up on the main road. She's go there and ring home. If Marcus answered she'd just ask for Richie. However, this walk was important. She'd set herself the target of reaching the lighthouse, which was still a good mile away. She picked up her pace and her body responded. There was plenty of life in her and she wanted to use it.

~

"I'd like to speak to Richie," she said as soon as she heard Marcus's smooth tones on the other end.

"Carol, where have you been?"

"Travelling."

"By bus, where's the pleasure in that?"

76

"I bought a car."

"What? Without my advice. I'd have thought—"

"Just put Richie on please."

"Don't talk for long, I'm expecting an important call from America."

Carol blew a raspberry down the line. Marcus took the receiver from his ear and frowned at it.

"Is there a fault?"

"Only with you. Now get Richie for me."

When he came on, he sounded tired.

"How are you?" she asked, holding the phone as tightly as she'd hug him if he was with her.

"Okay."

"School good?"

"Uha."

"You've settled in so quickly. So much change going to big school."

"Uha."

"I think about you a lot."

"Where did you go?"

"Away. I've got a cool car, you'll love it." Carol could just see it, resting by the old white establishment, glowing brightly amongst the grey tones of the gathering dusk. "We'll go for a ride."

"I thought you'd stay close to home."

"Home's where you make it. There's a big world beyond the end of the street. I want to see some of it."

"Isn't it frightening?"

"Sometimes. But exciting too. I go where the sky is blue."

He went silent like he did when he was thinking. She was sure he'd be biting a fingernail. Carol leaned against the inside of the box. There was a smell of damp and various spiders were competing for space in each square of glass. She threw in a few more coins to make sure they weren't suddenly disconnected.

"Are you going to forget about me, chasing the sun?" he enquired.

"No! Never! Whatever makes you think that? I'm just having a spell on my own."

"You didn't say goodbye."

Her chest tightened. Genuine hurt underlay his words. The call designed to help her separation was making it harder to bear.

"Things happened so quickly."

"You're right about that."

"I'm sure you're having some great times with daddy. You can watch all those boy programmes I used to complain about. And I bet you get more treats from him."

"Yeah. That's good, I guess. He won't wash my hair in the bath. And he doesn't check on me once I go to bed, so I read and lose track of time."

"How are you doing with Tolkien?"

"Finished the first book," he said with pride.

"I miss sharing it with you."

"Why not come back? Maybe you and dad could make up."

"I can't. He's probably changed the locks, knowing how careful he is. Besides, we just don't fit together any more. We did talk about this, remember?"

"Fiona comes round now. Sometimes she stays the night. She sleeps in your bed with dad. I don't like her very much."

"I'm sure she's very nice," Carol said, grinding her teeth.

"She tries to be. She's all girlie and wants to be my friend. Her perfume makes me sneeze."

"Oh, dear."

Carol had to suppress a giggle.

"And dad acts all weird when she's here, like everything has to be perfect for her."

"He wants you to be happy."

"They're always kissing. Makes me want to puke."

Me too, Carol thought. "I don't want to talk about him and her," she said.

"You chose to go because you hate dad now."

"Oh, Richie. There's more to it than that. More to me. I want to be surrounded by the life and love your father can't give me anymore. You and I can have plenty of that, as soon as I get settled."

He went quiet again. The telephone box closed around her like a metal vice. She sought the reassurance she needed to fight it off. "So you'll be all right?"

"I expect so. You always think things will work out nicely. Dad says we can go fishing this weekend."

"Great. Well, enjoy it and I'll ring again soon."

"Bye."

A deathly humming noise truncated their connection. Carol slumped to the ground. Her elation had been sucked from her, leaving an emptiness soon filled by doubts. She was wrong to be doing this when she had a child of school age. She was selfish and cruel. She was deluded to think anything might lie out there for her.

But she found the strength to leave the weight of her guilt behind, there and then. Up she had to get, and press on with her trip. The car called to her. She touched it like it was a rare sapphire as she passed by on the way back to her room. Tomorrow she would drive off again, keeping speed a part of the escape, marking out a direct line from the pain of the past.

CHAPTER ELEVEN

It was noise that caught her attention as she climbed from the Jensen and then, attracted by the rainbow of swirling lights, the crazy childhood memories came flooding back.

"A funfair," she gasped, walking onto the park towards a colourful arch that drew you in to a world of carousel chaos.

She lost herself in the experience and got thrown sideways, upside down and backwards until she screamed into the darkening sky, thrilled by the peril yet still glad she had worn trousers. On the big wheel she could reach out and touch branches of a large chestnut tree. The scent of oil filled her nostrils. She was celebrating being part of something without belonging to anything.

While the rock and roll blared from inadequate speakers, she tripped and manoeuvred past parents waiting for their children to return or groups of teenage boys who cursed and girls smelling of cheap perfume.

Her first date had been a trip to a place like this. As an impressible girl, that young rogue had persuaded her that his heart was as warm as his hands when they'd ended up out of sight behind the dodgems. So the opening kiss of her romantic life was accompanied by an intrusion beneath her clothing she had been unprepared for.

When she asked her mother if it was normal to be groped like that so soon in a relationship, it was held up as another example of her ongoing gullibility. "You can't always believe the best in people," mum had scolded, with dad nodding in agreement.

Carol finished with that particular boyfriend soon afterwards but made a few more similar mistakes before she found someone happy to hold hands for at least a month before getting physical.

A sticky sweet aroma drew her to a stall selling candy floss and popcorn. She always found the latter a more satisfying choice so ordered a big tub and set off around again; watching others shooting at cans or throw darts to win crappy prizes.

Eventually, her throat became dry and her head was dizzy from the clatter. Time to find some peace and quiet. She put the fluffy teddy she'd been awarded at the tombola into the car and headed on up the high street. The shops were closed now and their windows lit the empty pavements. Next to the formal town hall, a public house called Davy's Cellar invited in the passing traveller with candles burning in the windows and promises of fine wines within.

Carol didn't go into these places alone unless she was meeting someone. It wasn't that busy, which made her entrance more conspicuous. She kept her eyes down until she reached the bar and slipped quickly onto a stool to appear as if she'd been there the whole time.

"Martini and lemonade please," she said to a stony man serving.

He eyed her casually while he fixed her drink. Carol fidgeted and though her jumper was thin it stuck and prickled now she was in warm air. She did not want to engage in any sort of conversation with him about why she was there, so she made a brief scan of the surroundings and the clientele. At the nearest table a scruffy young chap was cradling a glass of whisky like it was a lover. Someone much smarter was regaling a small audience with details of his last sale and over the far side an old man was laughing to himself manically. Everyone was male.

"There you go. Fifty five pence."

Carol was surprised at the price. Then again, she was out of touch. She went too quickly to her purse for the money and succeeded only in spraying coins everywhere. She retrieved a few from the floor, aware that eyes were on her.

"Sorry," she said.

He shook his head and took his due before returning to the other end of the bar where a studious chap was scrutinising the newspaper. She listened to them as they exchanged political views. It was a dull conversation but she sat it out, feeling more likely to be left alone if she stayed put.

Now her focus was on not drinking too quickly. She'd had the courage to come in here so she was determined to brave it out. She took the opportunity to study the drinks on show. It was very rare for her to be anywhere like this so it was an education. She's never realised there were so many different types of whisky. Could the taste vary that much? A multitude of glasses stood in rows, some tatty looking menus lay in a pile and the memorial sheets of past customers were stuffed behind the till.

She didn't want to talk to anybody in here. The usual crowd in a pub reminded her too much of her early boyfriends; sad cases looking for an easy hit. So it was all the more remarkable to her when she engaged with the next complete stranger who walked in only ten minutes later. Perhaps the martini had gone to her head. It often did.

He was rugged looking with tight curly hair that had plenty of grey mixed in with black. His eyes were large and widened at each gulp of lager, beneath naturally raised brows. When he gave her a little smile his entire demeanour became ironic. Carol was uncertain how to react and ended up trying to ignore him.

However, it was difficult. He was two seats away and via the mirror behind the bar Carol was facing him directly. She found herself looking despite herself, which he noticed very quickly, and the more she did it the worse the predicament became. She thumped her empty glass down and swivelled out her chair. Time to get away.

"Can I get you another?"

He had spoken to her. She froze, facing his plaintive expression.

"What will it be?"

Carol twisted her features into disdain. "I don't think so, I have to go."

"To where?"

She wanted to explain she needed to find a place to stay the night, but knew that would give the wrong impression. In the end, she said nothing.

"Don't leave. Share a drink with me."

Every reason she had to answer in the negative had been left behind. And some chat would be welcome after several days alone.

"Just one. Then I'm off," she agreed.

"Fine with me. My name is Joe, by the way."

"Carol."

They joined hands for a brief shake. She noticed he had surprisingly slender fingers for such a big guy, stained with some kind of black dye. She climbed back into her seat and he crossed over to the one next to her, without asking. This was a bit imposing given he was quite a bulky specimen. However, she guessed if they were talking they should sit together.

"So?"

"I'm passing through," Carol explained.

He laughed and she noticed how raw it sounded. "I meant, what can I get you?"

"Oh!" Now Carol saw the joke. "Martini and lemonade."

"Same again," said the grumpy barman who was waiting for the answer.

"Make it a double," her new friend added.

"But—"

"No problem. Now you can tell me more. I've never seen you before and I'm here most nights."

Carol turned her head towards him without moving her body.

"I'm....travelling."

"Intriguing," he said, clenching his tongue and letting it slide out of sight again. "From where to where?"

Carol hesitated then went for it. "From my old life to a new one."

"Well, good on you!"

83

She thought he would mock, he had that sardonic air. His response was admirable.

"I've lived in this town all my life," he continued. "I don't cope with change. So I respect those who can."

"Thank you."

"So what do you do?"

Carol shrugged.

"I mean job wise. You're clearly not a housewife. You have to fund this free lifestyle?"

"I was."

"And now?"

She pushed out her bottom lip and appeared to not ever have considered such a question. "I used to be an estate agent," she offered without conviction.

"You could sell me a house," he said with a raising of his distinctive eyebrows.

She turned away and took a large slug of her drink.

"Does this new life involve having fun?" he asked.

She considered her response while she squeezed her hands together and then she nodded.

"So don't be angry with a man who appreciates you. I mean no harm."

Carol shuffled awkwardly in her chair. Her lack of confidence was making her cruel. Looking down she could see his strong arms resting on the bar as he turned his beer glass round and round on the mat.

"They are mighty fine tattoos," she said.

He held them up to give her a closer look. "Glad you like them."

"Do they have a meaning?"

"Of course. On the left we have snake symbols and a medusa. This is temptation. For the right I went for doves around a lion's head, to show strength and peace."

"So which one do you favour?"

"I am capable of both, like all of us. And don't forget this lady with serpents in her hair can represent female power and the male's fear of losing it, according to Freud. So it's complicated."

He was a lot more intellectual than he appeared. Worthy of more conversation.

"Was it an easy decision, having them done?"

"It's a kind of advertising because it is my job."

"Really?"

"Yep. Since leaving school."

"So you did those yourself?"

"No! It's delicate stuff. I got my then friend on it. I learned my trade from him."

"I've never had a tattoo," Carol said suddenly.

"Want one?"

"Oh, I don't know. I've never considered it."

"It adds beauty."

She saw herself in the mirror, smirking at the idea. "I could never have anything the size you've got."

"No. Small and subtle, that what the ladies ask for."

She turned and laid her cheek on her shoulder, fixing him with a pointed stare. "You could sort it for me?"

"Carol," he declared. "I can open up my parlour tonight for you."

His wait for her reply was awkward. When she downed her martini in one and stood up he presumed she was about to say goodbye.

"It could wait until tomorrow," he ventured. "Only it sounds like you're a girl in a hurry."

She seemed so grave he half expected a slap for his impudence.

"No. It must be now."

It was his turn to sink his drink quickly. Wiping his mouth with one hand he offered her the other. She took it gladly.

"Lead on," she purred.

CHAPTER TWELVE

Joe's parlour was small. With the shutters down, surrounded by large pictures of his previous work, Carol felt instantly claustrophobic. When he opened a large metal box containing his equipment she had the urge to leave.

"Those points look sharp," she said, with a nervous laugh.

Joe was soon next to her with his lightly mocking smile. He placed a hand on her shoulder and gave a little squeeze.

"I understand your anxiety. I see a lot of it. Even the biggest hard nuts that come in here wanting aggressive designs that pronounce their manhood to the world, they can be close to tears thinking about it."

"So it's going to hurt?"

"No denying that. But some areas are less sensitive than others."

Carol bit her lip. Did she have the courage? The new part of her, the carefree one that drove a big Jensen chanted in her head. "Do it, do it, do it!"

"I'll put some music on," Joe said.

While he was occupied, her thoughts raced. After they had been around the block ten times she came back to the inescapable truth. If she was going to stick to her crusade for change she had to get on with this. It would be her symbol of authenticity.

Dire Straits filled the room, the singer saying something about sweet surrender. Carol smiled.

"I'm ready."

Joe rubbed his hands together. "Okay. Where do you want it?"

"Excuse me?"

"You're tattoo."

"Oh!" Carol laughed at her misunderstanding. "I thought you meant...."

Joe appeared surprised though she was sure his innocence was fake.

87

"Never mind," she said. "I don't know. I hadn't exactly planned this."

"Well, what kind of design?"

Carol searched the walls for inspiration. Everything was big and bold.

"Small, very small," she decided.

"A name, a picture?"

Carol had to think quickly. Should it be Richie? To emphasise his importance. Yet she had just left him behind. The song was mentioning water. She'd never been comfortable in the water. She pulled her mouth out wide in comic desperation.

"Not sure."

"I'll show you some ideas. Here, sit."

He patted his padded table and they spent a while flicking through a catalogue he had of photographs and drawings. She noticed the delicate play of his fingers as he turned and touched each page with clear affection, holding his breath each time a new motif appeared and chewing his tongue. He cared about his art and what she thought of it.

"Roses are popular, a good warm colour," he suggested.

Carol thought back to the last few days. What had given her the biggest boost? The Jensen? An image of the car was too manly.

"Stars. A little collection of them, say five."

"Something like this," he wondered, turning to a specific page.

"Yes, only not so big."

"How about seven. The Seven Sisters. It's a constellation. Officially called Pleiades, from Greek mythology, the daughters of Atlas—"

"That'll be good," Carol said. His attention to detail was reassuringly overwhelming.

"And where?"

"On my back, right at the bottom."

"Let's get to it," he said, jumping up in eagerness.

88

"Oh fuck!" she breathed, holding her palms up to her cheeks. "The devil is in me."

"Lay flat on your front. You'll have to lift your jumper up a bit."

She did as he asked. He placed a warm palm on her skin.

"Is this the right place?"

She reached round and moved his hand lower. Together they reached the band of her jeans.

"Further," she resolved.

She raised her body enough to open the button and zip of her trousers and pull them down enough to expose the exact spot she had in mind.

"Here," he said, laying his fingers onto hers.

"Yes."

"Okay."

She relaxed as best she could. There was some cream he caressed into her skin. It felt good to be touched like that. The act of loosening her clothes and laying herself open to him was sensuous enough to shake off any last illusions of being a lady.

"Are you very sure? Getting one of these is easy, losing it again a lot harder."

She nodded and did not move. That was enough affirmation for him. A buzzing noise began and a punching sensation followed, like an injection. The pain was sharp from the start. She bit her lip until she was certain it was bleeding.

"Breathe, Carol," he advised.

She did as instructed. It was difficult. She was tense. Her ribcage was squashed flat against the table even though it was soft. She only managed short, shallow bursts.

He made conversation so help keep her mind occupied. "So where are you off to next?"

"No idea."

89

"Think you might go back to the old life?"

"I can't."

"I see. Not in any way?"

"I wouldn't let myself."

"So this is as permanent as you're tattoo."

"I have a son," she said, with a wince.

"How old?"

"Eleven."

"You're leaving him too?"

"No. He'll have to come to me, on visits. He prefers to be with my husband. Correct that, ex-husband....his dad."

"How hard is that?"

"Extremely."

"Things haven't worked out with your marriage?"

He was being very direct. She might usually have ended this kind of questioning. Tonight, she was glad to talk.

"They did. He's found someone younger now."

"Oh dear."

"It's been a kind of wake up call. It's made me realise I become boring, complacent, too....passive."

"Sounds like you've been suffering."

"Except. These past few days have been the happiest I've had in so long. I'd forgotten what it was like. So it must be right."

"I'm pleased for you."

Carol marvelled at the change that had come over her. Lying in a seedy parlour, late in the night, allowing a stranger access to her body, openly discussing her private life. You could only call it brave or stupid. She favoured brave. A feather in her new hat.

90

Even the pain was oddly pleasurable, like giving birth. When Richie arrived, the intensity was beyond her anticipated imagination. Tonight another creation was being formed, unique to her, springing from a whim.

"The small of your back is very beautiful," Joe said.

She laughed. "I bet you've used that line a few times!"

"I mean it."

"You didn't save those words for me. I am naive but I know I'm not the first."

"Maybe not. Still true though. Your skin is very smooth."

So are you, she thought. It was nice.

"Tell me about some of your old flames," she requested.

"There's not been that many."

"But a few? Anyone special?"

"I try and forget."

"Come on, I've told you plenty. Now it's your turn."

He sighed. It was more like a deep growl. The memories were clearly brought a twinge of agony.

"Okay. Once. A girl called Kirsty. Very fit she was."

"Good looking you mean?"

"No, fit as in jogging and gym fit. And a stunner. She did make up, so we had a bit in common, decorating people. And we loved going to the theatre together."

"Sounds an excellent match."

"She ran off with a guy called Peter."

"I'm sorry."

"I couldn't understand it. He was a fat bloke. I guess he must have had hidden qualities. I had been very loyal to her. That might be my fault. I let myself go as well after that and have never really made an effort since."

He stopped working when he noticed Carol was crying.

"I'll give you a moment. We're almost done. I don't want to think I'm hurting."

"Carry on," she urged. "It's not the needle."

He continued, glancing when he could and frowning in concern.

"Why the suffering?" he asked, eventually.

Carol's damp face lightened with a smile. "Oh, I was reflecting on the bitterness of life. How often dreams are dashed. How brief delight is."

"Don't fill your head with sadness tonight," he said.

"Sorry," she sniffed. "I'm getting my silly tears on your table."

The machine ceased its buzzing and she felt his hand stroke her neck. She closed her eyes and he carried on, filling his fingers with her hair and brushing away the melancholy.

"They sure are pretty coloured panties," he observed.

For a moment she was startled. Then she saw this as the perfect opportunity to put a seal on this outrageous adventure.

"Pull my trousers down and you can see them better."

She held her breath again. He did it slowly, sensually. Then there was a pause. She imagined him taking in the view of her, barely covered by the see through lace.

"Do they feel as soft as they look?" he asked.

"Only one way to find out."

While his fingers explored she eased herself into a warm pool of arousal. She knew her chest would be flushed by it and when he went beneath the material, down into the crack between her legs, he found she was damp with expectation. She rolled onto her back and he moved across the top of her.

"Not here," she whispered, laying her hand on his chest.

"My flat's upstairs," he suggested.

"No. Not a place you've been with someone else. Come out in my Jensen. We'll find an isolated spot and get in the back. It's tight and secluded there and that car makes me feel so sexy."

92

CHAPTER THIRTEEN

He was a big guy, grown large on a diet of lager and fried food, so it not easy to creep into the cramped bedroom with the breakfast. A stubbed his toe made him curse and Carol stirred.

Her eyes had to adjust to the light dawning through thin curtains. As the haze of slumber faded she saw Joe's amused face and instantly recalled their intense intimacy in the night.

She had allowed this man to fill her with his pleasure. On the back seat, with her legs so high and wide she could touch the roof with her toes, her insides burned in glory.

"I'm going to explode," he had gasped.

"Me too!" she cried.

The missile hit its mark, the dust settled and he had held her tight. There were no awkward manoeuvres, no feeling dirty, only his sweet whispers and a reassuring anonymity in the darkness of that car park. Nothing intruded on their moment of intimacy. The big teddy bear she had won at the fair watched in impassive silence, his jolly grin unchanged.

And now here was a tray of corn flakes, a boiled egg, some toast and coffee, decorated by a plastic rose. She sat up to receive his gift and grabbed a deep breath while she took it all in.

"I'm sorry it's so early, but I have to get the parlour open and I didn't want you to wake up to nothing."

"Joe, that's so sweet."

She reached out and caressed his cheek as he sat on the edge of the bed beside her. He was wearing a dressing gown and where it had fallen open, a tattoo of a man crying was visible on his chest.

"That was quite a night," he said, with eyebrows arched.

Carol giggled. "Yes, wasn't it just?"

"You're a fine woman Carol."

His eyes strayed down from her face and when she followed their path she saw how her naked breasts sat proudly exposed above her breakfast. She went instinctively to cover them and then laughed.

"I think it's a bit late to worry!" she said.

She set about eating and remembered how much of an appetite enthusiastic sex gave her. He looked very pleased that his food was appreciated.

"Didn't have any real flowers so I nicked one from the display in the parlour window. I think the sun has faded it a bit over the years."

"I don't mind. No one has given me anything like it for so long."

"And I haven't had a good time with a woman for even longer."

"Amazing what buying one drink can get you."

She winked at him and then suddenly her chewing slowed. Her eyes narrowed on a point somewhere in the clutter of the room.

"Oh my god," she gasped.

"What is it?"

"I broke the law!"

"What we did is no crime."

"No, not that! I drove, last night. After drinking, I drove. First here, then out and back again. I never gave it a second thought!"

She dropped her cutlery and pressed a palm to her mouth.

"You weren't that—"

"No excuses, Joe. I've always hated people who do that."

"It's not—"

"What is happening to me? Freedom is one thing, but stupidity is too much. I have a child. Leaving him behind was rough enough, he doesn't need to mourn me and know I've killed someone because I'm selfish."

"Calm down, Carol," Joe urged.

She felt she wanted to throw the tray aside, leap up out of bed and run away from this, herself and the memory. Only his firm hands on her shoulders made her stop and think rationally.

"It was all part of what you needed," he told her. "Going into that bar, spending the night with a stranger. Just accept what you drank was essential. Now it's done and you feel bad, that's natural too. But your here safe with me now and you care like hell that you drove that car when you were a bit pissed."

Carol sighed and accepted the sincerity staring into her eyes. "Yes, you're right, I do care. And that means I'm not the complete rebel I thought I might have been. I'm an act. Not a very convincing one."

He released her and sat back again, conscious that the indent of his fingers was visible on her skin.

"Which is why I must leave this morning," she announced.

He looked completely crestfallen. She bit her lip and continued.

"This has been delightful but I have to let it go for now. I think there is more for me to discover. I'm not yet ready to have reached any great conclusions. I want to go out there, feel the wind in my hair and hear the music it makes."

Joe traced the pattern on the duvet with his forefinger and all the lines seemed to go in circles. "You're fortunate," he said. "To have that to reach for."

"What's to stop you doing the same?"

He snorted. "I'm not one for adventures. Everything I need I have here. My parlour, my friends, my past and you, for the moment."

"You could come with me."

He began chewing his tongue again. "Except," he concluded. "You don't really mean that do you? I'd cramp your style, be like a trap, stop the unravelling of that free spirit."

"I'm sorry," Carol said, not for anything specific.

Both took a minute to consider the future, while an energetic robin sang from a tree on the street below.

"Think of me out there, looking for answers, getting lost and all the while you've found contentment in one place. Who's the more fortunate?"

"Carol, I've waited a long time for another Kirsty. Now I've found her and I won't be getting to see her tomorrow, or maybe never. And yes I'll sit at the bar and imagine you, in the back of that fancy car with some other lucky bloke, and my heart will be scattered."

"No! That's not me. I don't indulge in casual sex."

He tipped back and the irony was on his face again. "Oh, really?"

"Oh, stop it. What we had last night was special."

"So why are you running away?" he bellowed.

His outburst startled her. She was used to the measured smart ass that was Marcus.

"Because I care for you," she sighed.

He shrugged in confusion.

"I want to stay, believe me. All this is nice, better than I've had. But what you said was right. I actually left my old life less than a week ago. It's too soon to settle into a new one. I'll be restless and start treating you badly and you don't deserve that. Or I'd be looking down the road and wondering what might have been there."

Joe did not answer. He stood up, removed the tray and left the room. It seemed to indicate that he accepted her explanation. She hoped as much while she searched around for her clothes. Freshening up in the bathroom, she paused before the smeared mirror to check out the woman on the other side.

Her eyes still begged to please; only now it was aimed at her. There was determination in those sharp lines and substance behind the bone. She had the credentials to survive alone.

Was she sure? Or had she struck lucky early? Maybe by going she would head only into ruin. The uncertainty was terrifying and liberating at the same time. This was what teenage had been like, soaring and dropping through emotional states. She craved that old excitement so she opted for the wonder of the unexpected.

Joe was busy in his parlour when she came down, writing figures into a battered old journal. She hesitated. She had to say a proper goodbye. Would he grant her that?

"I'm....off," she murmured.

He looked up and stared at her for much longer than was comfortable.

"Say something," she urged, twisting the handles of her bag through her fingers.

He slapped the pen down and began to rifle through the drawer beside him, emerging with a card which he brought over and handed to her.

"My number," he said, with a serious expression. "If and when your great trip gets you down, call me."

"Okay, I will."

"Perhaps. I'm not going to expect it, just hope for it."

She brushed her fingers across his business logo of a serpent twisted around a heart and smiled, looking up to his solid frame as he stood close.

"Though I'm scared to leave you, I'm comforted to know you'll be there when I run into trouble."

He turned his head on one side as if expecting more.

"Not fair, though is it?" she admitted. "The way this works, you can't contact *me* for the same reasons."

"I'll still have you close," he said, holding his shoulders back. "Your name is going to be inked into my skin." He pointed to a spot below his collar bone. "Just about here, above my heart."

"Poor sweet Joe." She touched his stubbly face once more. "I'm not used to being the rogue."

"Don't feel bad," he told her. "You're the product of what you were. Life has made you this way."

She gulped back her sentimental emotions.

"Go," he instructed, kissing the top of her head and returning to his desk. She waited for a moment until she realised he would not look up again. With a furrowed brow he kept his head lowered. She glanced around the parlour at the artistic images of dragons, snakes, mermaids, roses, and at the big metal box that housed his tools. There was his soft table where she had laid with her arse exposed to his soft touch. Would she ever see any of this again?

She dare not linger for the risk of giving in was strong. The old Carol was not yet buried. So she stepped briskly outside. The world was a curious mixture. The sun was strong, illuminating the rain that fell gently in a curtain of shiny dampness. A wave of doubt threatened to crush her where she stood until she saw the car, parked right outside and ready for action. After a wistful glance into the back, picturing herself spread-eagled beneath Joe's mighty weight, she sank into the leather driving seat and felt the strong gear stick in her palm. With a roar she took off, carving through the timid traffic and out where the road was wide and straight. The engine purred happily, a reassuring and satisfying light shudder energised her bones. She drove for miles without any idea of direction or purpose. To keep moving was the answer. It was only when she stopped, hemmed in by a town square surrounded by ornate buildings, that she looked in the rear view mirror and saw the tears streaming down her cheeks.

CHAPTER FOURTEEN

The street lamp threw its light across the room and on to Carol's back as she turned, naked, to see Joe's work. Seven sisters clustered in neat unison, dark and still a little sore, against her white skin. She nodded her approval. It had been worth the pain, bringing siblings she wished she'd had, romantic mystery and a story to tell.

She headed on into the bathroom and sank into the tub of foamy water. Her limbs betrayed the tension of the day. She had challenged her uncertainty with the spark of the dynamic future she pictured. The testing of the path was enough in itself to bring belief.

"Time to slow down," she sighed, stretching out until her heels reached the plug. "Thank you, Joe."

She missed him. He'd be in that bar now, drinking his lager. She hoped he was with friends. She hoped she had not changed him. She wanted him to always use those soft fingers to create beauty. He was so gentle.

Later, she sat beside the open window with a glass of wine and watched the busy town going about its business. There was enough of a chill in the air to make most people hurry; only the young defied the elements and hung around on corners trying to win favour with laughter.

It was safer for her up here. Detachment, she decided, was the best approach for a while, to take stock of her wishes and woes. The world moved so fast you could get out of tune with yourself too easily and your intentions might get lost. Tomorrow she wanted to try out her newly freed mind on some culture.

~

In the gallery she found reds and golds that drew her in close and sent her to the library to find out more about each artist's life. This was not enough. She wanted more of the emotions they felt and so found books that moved her, devouring the words on park benches or lying out across her bed.

She would go for drives in the Jensen, playing new music to tear and heal on the wonderful 8-track stereo. Her journeys took her to a ruined abbey where she wandered and saw beautiful new roses that made her think of Joe, springing from between the cold stone. She moved on. At a fine castle, built with great purpose and the need to survive, she gazed down from the battlements upon the rooftops of the town, proud to be free of the strife contained below.

There had never been enough time for this when she was with Marcus and Richie. She did not consider her needs. So she unfolded into a second childhood, every bit as fresh and baffling as her first. Until, after two weeks of fulfilment and a hotel bill that required a visit to the bank to clear, she went on again.

~

She'd drove off early that morning, skipping the usual indulgent breakfast at the hotel, and she fought condensation on the windows without success. Pulling over into a lay-by, she slumped into the deep seat and exhaled deeply, steaming the windows even more.

Maybe the air vents were blocked or the fan had stopped working. She'd never been much good at controlling such things, as Marcus was often reminding her. She was frustrated. Her chariot wasn't leading her to victory today. It was going to take significant effort and willpower. She reached out and wrote her name on the moist glass beside her, as if needing to understand who she was.

"Where to go?" she wondered.

Twisting round, she focused on the soft, brown teddy sitting on the back seat. He still had that cheerful smile. Nothing seemed to bother him.

"Any ideas?" she asked. There was no response.

She had a map book in her bag, which she had not consulted since setting out. Now seemed the optimum moment to start. The interior of the car was large by modern standards, but even with the chair pushed back, she was struggling with the big pages. She got out and spread it on the huge bonnet.

The problem, she soon realised, is that all the maps in the world can't help unless you have some idea of where you are in the first place. The town she'd left was called Ilminster and had since been travelling east....?
She turned full circle to try and work out where the sun had come up. Unfortunately the grey clouds cemented out all differentials in light. This wasn't getting any easier. Perhaps drifting aimlessly was better. She laid herself across the bonnet to get closer to the detail. If she was where she guessed, there were plenty of places in each direction.

The sound of a loud horn from a passing truck shattered all concentration. The grinning thumbs up she got from the driver momentarily confused her until she realised he was showing appreciation of her, spread over a car in tight jeans. The old Carol would have been put out by this intrusion. Now she laughed and waved, receiving a second toot for the willingness to play her part in the oldest game in the world. The big orange letters along the side of this lorry advertising tea also mentioned Andover.

"Okay, I'll follow signs to Andover," she decided.

When she got there she considered the reasons for this decision over a tall cup of coffee. She didn't want easy options, she was too ambitious for that. Many of those books and paintings had been inspired by Europe. A romantic idea stirred around her mind. You could repeat this whole crazy trip on a bigger canvas. Venice. Or Cordoba. She'd seen pictures of Cordoba in a magazine. It was beautiful there. The possibilities were endless.

A very thin pianist was entertaining the cafe with some jaunty noodling. No one seemed to hear his playing anymore than they noticed him wince between each piece and rub his aching hands. She didn't want to disappear into nothing like this.

101

At the next table two ladies came to sit down together. When one pushed the sugar bowl to the other, the recipient responded with a loud 'no!', like she was offended. Perhaps she was proud of her ability to resist? Or afraid she might not? Or maybe making a point? Carol shook her head. Nothing was simple.

She tapped her spoon on the cup. A woman was just leaving with her child. Before they opened the door to the keen, cold breeze, she crouched down and pulled his coat tightly around him, enclosing his cute face in a fluffy hood.

Carol knew she wasn't ready to be without Richie for too long. Wherever her wheels had taken her these last few weeks, he'd remained a major cog she had to fit in with. If she was hiding beneath a thick the veil of guilt, he could lift it. She'd spoken to him again only last night and when she heard the child in his voice she could see him in her head. He was disoriented, like her absence was making him doubt the path ahead.

She could not go back to living in that house. She was too changed. Her departure was one of life's lessons for Richie to learn. It was bound to be hard, however much he gravitated towards his clever father. But Cordoba and Venice could wait, at least until he was older. There was still one part of her old self she needed to be.

~

The night fell quicker than she expected. As she'd drifted away from the main routes the darkness closed all around and the focus became the road ahead, illuminated by the headlights. Her travel bag on the passenger seat, was a reminder of her rootless state, her only companion if you discounted the silent teddy in the back.

A sad song came on the radio, the words pinning her down uncomfortably. When she tried to sing along, the signal weakened into a scratchy static, only to return with the crunching punch line. She waited for the presenter to identify the track, only to miss it on another roar of nothing. Slumping over the wheel, doubt filled her head, deep enough to fuel the panic of uncertainty.

"Stop, stop!" she exclaimed in a rush of breathy emotion.

Being in this remote valley as the last person alive didn't offer much hope. The search for herself had led her to lose touch with everyone else. She wanted to be known again, recognised. When the moon peeked from behind a cloud the landscape brightened, encouraging her to get out and take in some air.

In the silvery light she made out the shape of a horse's head, with ears pricked and curious. Going closer made it gallop off beyond sight. She thumped the fence post in frustrated disappointment.

This was like those days at home as a child when her parents went out, leaving her to find her own sources of amusement. What had she done then? Usually, she went to the park and followed her friend Melody around. She was the leader of their local pack. The girls would all join hands and feel stronger as a unit.

The sound of a car approaching interrupted her recollection. She watched the lights come near and hoped whoever was driving would stop and chat. After they had gone past without even hesitating, the instinct to follow grabbed her. Virtually falling back in to the Jensen, she got it started and headed off in pursuit.

A chase ensued. Each time she got close to the bumper, her quarry accelerated away, only to slow down again and let her catch up. This went on for fifteen miles. When they reached a long, downward stretch she let her vehicle show its drag strip performance, sailing past her competitor with ease. She got so far ahead there was time to stop at the next crest, get out again and wait for a rendezvous that now had to happen. But instead of making her acquaintance, the new friend whizzed by, leaving only a slight impression of a male at the wheel anxious to remain unknown.

103

She kicked at the stones around her feet. This was going to be another night alone. The glow of a distant town beckoned. But stepping inside her beloved automobile she felt the cockpit's embrace as the reassuring smell of leather drew her down. Caressing the accelerator with her dusty shoe made some of the dials wave a friendly needle at her.

They would sleep together, out here beyond the demands of the world, with the moon as a guardian. Tomorrow was a different day, as she drifted slowly closer to Richie, when her roaming spirit needed to put down some kind of marker and claim a base from which to direct future voyages.

CHAPTER FIFTEEN

Sleep was spasmodic. The sky began to lighten. She would have liked to have rolled around in a luxury bed, let her limbs unravel listlessly. This wasn't one of her nice hotel rooms. She was curled up on the back seat of a fantastic vehicle that was a dream to drive but not designed for slumber. She went outside to pee while it was still dark enough to remain unseen. Not that there was likely to be other people up here on the hills at this hour. A dog was barking, probably from a distant farm. She took the opportunity to change her underwear. It was cold with the wind blowing around her naked backside and new tattoo so she hurried back to the car as spots of rain added to the discomfort.

Breakfast consisted of the remains of some cake and a carton of orange juice. She combed her hair in the rear view mirror and applied a bit of lipstick. The same jumper and jeans would do. Armed with her best smile she set off down into the valley.

The road meandered down between high hedges, cutting off the landscape, the grass in the centre eventually disappearing as she reached a T-junction. So for the hundredth time she had to weigh up the merits of two unknown directions. Left or right, high or low? The signpost offered two separate villages, with similar names, each three miles away. There was no compunction to decide quickly as she was the only one there.

She gripped the wheel and felt the hum of the engine. Was there a message coming from the Jensen, was it nudging her to take a particular route? Did the indicator make a more positive noise in the up position or down? Nothing was talking to her today. Until a robin caught her eye as it landed on the fence opposite.

"Well?" she asked. "Do you have a clue for me?"

The bird, a fine specimen she thought, seemed to look at her very intently as if making sure of whom she was. It then began an excited chirping and tail flicking dance in which the nod of the head and twitch of the beak pointed to her right. After a minute or two, she forced her transfixed state into action and turned as suggested.

"Thank you," she called, giving the robin a wave, which looked suitably astonished.

The first sign of gathered civilisation she came to was a new estate. In fact, part of it was still being built. A large sign advertised perfect homes for sale and had a picture of a beautiful white family looking absolutely delighted with their life in a smart fresh place.

She followed the big purple arrow and a set of little flags to a neat office with large windows and lots of full flower beds outside. When she went in, she was greeted by a tall man with a ready smile and a suit that was clearly one size too small. In fact, he was larger than life, with a big head resting on a big neck that strained against the collar of his shirt. He was rubbing his hands together in eagerness.

"Madam, how can I help you today?"

"I want to buy a house," she said.

He glanced at her attire. Boots, jeans and a baggy jumper, ruffled from a night in the car. His eyes strayed over her shoulder to the Jensen parked outside. She was being assessed for potential wealth.

"We do offer a ninety five percent mortgage if—"

"Don't need one, I'll pay in full in cash."

This stunned the false smile off his face. He drew himself up to full height and blinked repeatedly.

"Can I look at the show home?" she enquired.

He shook himself into action with a gesture to walk off through the front, while searching his pockets for keys. The sales pitch began immediately. It used to be her profession so she knew how to ignore the customary verbiage. She didn't care that they'd won home of the year award or how many such developments were in progress across the country. Even the

106

specification of the materials, the colours chosen and all the guarantees anyone might wish for had no effect on her.

His voice continued to purr through the superlatives while she assessed for herself. Did this feel like home? Could she see future moments playing out in the rooms? Was there space for Richie to stay? Were the patios all as secluded as this?

All the answers came back positive. This was close enough to the old family house without being too much so. It was time to slow down. The deal was done.

"I'm impressed with your sense of purpose, madam," the overblown estate agent had concluded.

She was too. With the same power of instant resolve she walked away with a place to live as quickly as she'd bought the car.

~

"Well, do you like it?"

Carol watched Richie carefully taking in the new surroundings. His cheeks had flushed as she would have expected. This was a big, new experience, coming to her house after they'd been apart for so long. She saw the spectre of Marcus trying to break out in the boy in the form of strong brow and chin. He fidgeted as his eyes rolled around the confines of this new space.

Carol kept on talking to hide her nerves. "I'm sorry if it's seemed to take a while. The paperwork and stuff is—"

"I know, dad explained the whole thing."

"Oh."

His tone remained harsh. She was curious to know what Marcus might think but wished she wasn't still infected by him, so avoided probing further.

"I took the time to choose colours and furnishings, getting ideas," she said, still trying to get a positive reaction.

107

He was standing in the room she'd planned for him to make his own. Apart from a bed the whole thing had been left empty as a blank canvas to complete.

"This is what you wanted?" he asked.

"The house do you mean?"

"The whole thing."

Carol leaned against the doorframe for support. "Once your father decided to leave me, I knew I had to get away, find a new dream."

He scratched his face with obvious agitation. "Your dream," he said.

"Okay, that's true," she admitted. "What else would you have had me do? Your dad let me go like one of his business contracts. It was too painful to hang around."

"Pain for everyone," he commented.

She went to him and took his hand. "I've missed your bony fingers," he confessed, lifting them up to see.

"Thank you," she said. "I've missed everything about you."

"I thought I might have lost you."

"Never."

The hug that ensued was strong and tight. He was being characteristically strong but Carol felt sure he was crying inside his streaky frame. Twelve was too tender an age for all this crap.

"Have you had fun?" he asked, watching her face as closely as she did his.

"I've had a blast. Lots of time to do as I please."

"You can still do that, with me."

"Yes, of course. Except I will have to get a job. Most of the money has gone."

He began to walk around with a bit more focus, looking out the window to take in the view of rows of places like hers.

"There enough left for a shopping spree. We can go and get you lots of stuff for in here. It'll be my birthday present to you, make up for not being there last month. You can choose what you like."

She saw his grin for the first time that day. He was astonishingly attractive, like Marcus, when he smiled.

"Does that mean we can go out in the car again?" he wondered.

"Of course."

"Yipeee!"

He bounced past her with arms aloft, heading out to the drive.

"I didn't think you liked it?" she said. "You had such a long face from the moment I picked you up."

"Mum. I love your motor! I want to keep going out in it, over and over. Can you pick me up from school, so my friends can see?"

Carol hooted. "Whatever!"

They climbed in together. He looked so small in the passenger seat, torn between gazing at all the controls and watching the world speed by. He had to sit up very straight to see out over the bonnet.

"Cool!" he chimed.

He waved to people walking around the town. The spirit of the child had survived his parent's divorce. Carol hoped it was a sign that he would be able to endure all the rotten things life was bound to dish him.

"Let's open the sun roof," she suggested.

"Mum, it's December."

"Who cares, let's have some excitement. I did the same one night when I was sleeping on the back seat. You could see the stars, moving across the sky, I was staring at them for hours."

His laugh was a little nervous. "You've changed, mum."

"For the better?"

"Mostly."

"Good."

109

"This is so much better than dad's boring car," he said.

Carol smiled briefly. Inside she was punching the air. The Jensen Interceptor had brought her great triumph. She ran the steering wheel through her palms and hoped it felt her love.

The child sat back into the soft leather and absorbed the great view through the open roof. Up into the blue he soared, above the restricting buildings, until he was higher than the jets that left streaky white lines across the sky. The music was loud, guitars roared and the harmonies were simultaneously tight and loose. The sun would always be shining in timeless, directionless moments like this. Perhaps if you could just keep on going the troubles would not catch up with you.

CHAPTER SIXTEEN

Time spent with mum was always best when that sun roof was open. He could share her freedom, both would hold an arm up into the onrushing wind, each feeling the air on their face and having to squint into the sun. Back on the ground Richie struggled, plagued by uncertainty he was unable to share with his super confident father or his new plaything Fiona who treated him like a five year old. His friends suffered from similar angst, too ready to suggest drastic action they themselves would never take.

This left his mother. She was so upbeat and ready to accept whatever fate kept hidden while he was conditioned to expect only difficulties and disappointment. Her new carefree nature was perplexing and he often sat on the sofa at home deep in thought, watching the clouds scudding past and chewing his fingers until they bled.

"I can't work out what I want to do," he'd often moan when she'd sit by his bed on the nights he stayed with her.

"Give it time. Be young and quit worrying," was her common answer.

Except he didn't stay young or feel young for very long. Ongoing success at school built up to ever pressing questions about the future. His father came home early one evening to find him and his friends playing poker and smoking instead of revising for his exams. The ensuing row led him to ring his mum to hastily arrange a sleep over at hers to escape the bad atmosphere. He sat on the castellated wall at the end of the drive, waiting for the sound of that big engine.

"I'm seventeen and having a personal crisis I daren't share with my parents," he complained. His like minded audience, who had stayed with him, listened while they all stared into the dark evening.

"I have a father very sure I need to join him on his business crusade to relieve the world of all its money. A mother with a wild spirit all of her own and a over eager willingness to trust. Neither way suits me."

111

"Go your own way, man," one of them advised.

"But to do that I need to find something I believe in and then trust that. I've tried religion, the supernatural, classical literature. And love just seems way too difficult. Nothing feels quite right. So many possibilities that all lead back to the same empty room with nowhere to hide."

"It's a drag," they agreed. "Who's got the energy for all that?" another said.

The beautiful blue Jensen rolling up the gravel drive was a relief. The reprieve would only be temporary, he'd have to be back tomorrow for school. He jumped down with his bag and gave his mates a thumbs up.

"Take it easy," one of them called.

He stopped and wondered what taking it easy might be like. Growing up to this point had been nothing but hard.

~

His mum rescued him again in that all conquering car on the day of his graduation.

He had, like many other bright teenagers with good exam results, continued on up the educational ladder to university, putting off the time when he would have to stop learning and try out real life. In the process he discovered drugs and the short term pleasures of sex. None of these things were conducive to finding a vocational path and his father was giving him a hard time over it when she had turned up in a short summer dress, with a bright smile and many congratulations. His dad was distracted by her brown legs and Richie loved it that she had upstaged Fiona.

He enjoyed seeing his parents being civil to one another but after the fanfare of the parade died away he was left with having to make the next step. He gravitated towards his mother. Arriving at her little fortress of a home, pulling up next to her sleek vehicle in his clapped out little Ford, he found she was packed and ready for a new adventure.

~

"So you're going again?" he observed, seeing her cases in the hall.

112

"I promised myself I would, as soon as you'd graduated," she said, pausing at the bottom of the stairs. "I can't let myself down."

"And me?"

"Richie. I've not lied to you. I assured you I'd be around until you were your own man. You've got all the tools you need now."

"Fine."

His voice was clipped and tight, stomach knotted. She was busy but could never deny him her attention. He was much taller now and she had to look up and gauge his mood.

"Has your dad been on your back again?"

"Completely. He came all the way up there to confront me."

"Oh, I see." She rubbed her hands anxiously down the front of her dungarees. "Let's take some coffee onto the patio and talk about it."

He went out and waited for her, watching the neighbours washing flap in the breeze, the sun bringing no warmth. She appeared soon enough with a tray of treats. He took a biscuit and bit on it aggressively.

"Tell me then," she requested.

He hunched forward and focused on ground, thinking back to the recent encounter when he came home from work to find his father sitting on the steps of the flat, in a dark raincoat, looking very determined.

"Do you think a job at a fish canning factory is the best use for sixteen years of schooling?" he said, without getting up, holding up his arm to display his expensive watch. "If you work this late you should be making a fortune."

"Ask me how I am," Richie replied.

"How are you?"

"Grand, thanks."

"You might be physically well, but mentally you've got problems."

"Oh, really?"

"You need to get on board with the world before it passes you by."

"I feel trapped by the system."

He had a clear answer. "In order to stop this skulking you have to get out there and start competing."

"When I'm ready."

"So this is leading somewhere?"

"I guess."

"That mad mother of yours is poisoning your mind."

"She's happy. You saw how great she looked at the graduation."

He gave him a quizzical look before standing up and smoothing out his raincoat with leather gloved hands.

"I was pleased she hadn't turned completely hippy. But let's not talk about her. I'm here to make sure you don't go astray. If you need money to set you off, you just need to ask. I won't leave you stranded."

"I want to do it myself, my way," Richie explained.

He held his father's eyes until he was sure he understood.

"Well, I have much business to attend to. A fortune isn't made sitting still wondering what everything means. Don't waste your potential for too long."

"He left then, mum. Shook my hand and went. Didn't even come in for a while."

Carol turned her mug around in her hand while she pictured the two of them together like that. "He cares," she concluded. "You can't ever accuse him of not supporting us, financially. The problem is he's lost touch with the human things you need as well."

While Richie clamped his teeth on his thumb, Carol stretched out and put her feet up on an empty chair.

"So he thinks I'm mad, does he?"

"You took him by surprise when he saw you, though. You weren't the dull housewife he left behind."

"He's always been swayed by looks. Two dimensional as ever."

"Cardboard."

"He believes you get what you deserve by hard work. With his sharp mind and flashy smile, he's done very well for himself. In the process, my needs, and yours, got overlooked."

Richie waved his hand. "I shouldn't let him get to me. I wish I could please him as me rather than who he wants me to be."

She nodded. "I think that's what I thought towards the end of our marriage." He smiled at their shared experience and took a large swig of coffee. "Well, I guess we won't change him now."

His remark was very true and they both nodded but only one of them had truly come to terms with that fact and she was the one with the wings to fly.

~

"You're going so far away this time. What will I do when I need to talk?" They were washing up after sharing lunch. "We'll write a lot. You can really sort your thoughts out in a letter and lie much easier. It has a lot of merits. I had someone I met at school who moved away. We kept in touch as pen friends for years until she found a boy to love."

He shook his head. "I'm not sure I like the way you describe it. You can lose touch with a person."

"We won't," she assured him.

He wandered around the room drying a plate with vigour. "How long will you travel for this time, do you think?"

"Can't say. I want to work my across Europe until I either like somewhere enough to stay longer term or get fed up and return here."

"Can anyone live that way?"

"I can get the odd job, fruit picking, waitressing, to pay for some of the cost. The rest is the small remainder of what I got out of your father."

"Sounds risky."

"I'll give it a try."

He remained uneasy. He was the youth, the one meant to show the old how fixed they'd become in their ways. Yet it was her who was still growing, on a

115

chase for setting moons, hungry for new sensations, without concern. In a completely different manner, she highlighted his inadequacies as much his father.

Admiration was there too. He glanced at the brochures piled on the table. Exotic locations; Venice, Cordoba, Dubrovnik, Budapest, the Amalfi Coast, Scandinavian fjords and white peaks in the Alps. The list was endless. She'd never run out of options, such was the burning desire to explore.

"So no regrets leaving this place? You were so thrilled to have a little house of your own."

She was busy disposing of uneaten food from the fridge and didn't miss a beat. "I've been here ten years and all of them good but nothing compares with the road ahead. A while back, when I first left, I stood out under the stars in complete darkness. I never did that at home. I could see millions of miles, deep into space. There were suns, planets, each with a story of their own. The Universe is so vast. I can't stay in one place. Even in this little corner, I have to get out there and investigate. I won't have any regrets."

He guessed as much. Except she paused then, and looked deep into her memory.

"Maybe one," she sighed.

He was keen to know more.

"You see that memo board behind you. That business card pinned to the corner. He's an angel I'll be leaving behind."

Richie read the name Joe's Parlour and saw the heart encircled by a snake.

"I've looked at this many times. You told me he was the one who did your tattoo."

"He was," she said, coming up alongside him and touching the raised motif gently. "He was also a lovely man who wanted to be with me."

"So what happened to stop that? Not much holds you back these days."

116

"It was all too soon after I left your father. I told Joe I'd call just as soon as I settled down."

"But you didn't?"

"Call or settle down?"

Richie shrugged. Carol laughed.

"Neither, I guess! But I feel badly about him. The independence was important to me and however hard the longing or loneliness got it was never enough to make me give in to temptation and dial that number."

"You seem happy enough to me," he said.

"You can't live your life for someone else. I learned that."

He put a long arm around her. "Make sure you stick to that principle and look after yourself. You'll stand out with that car. Don't be too nice, it's a fault of yours."

"This is role reversal," she observed.

"Not sure that's a good thing, for me, at least. What's it say about my ambition?"

"You have to take care, wherever you are."

They faced each other now, holding hands the same way as on his first visit here.

"I'm ready to go," she said.

The lines on her face were all upturned and her hair flowed long with the sort of freedom she exuded.

"And I should get back. I'm on an early shift tomorrow."

"Wish me luck."

"I do."

"I read something somewhere that you can measure how much you love someone by how much your heart breaks when you have to part."

His perfectly carved cheeks were unmoving. "I love you a lot."

"I'm hurting too," she assured him. "I wish I could slip away unnoticed, make this easier for you."

"You could make it better, you know."

"How?"

"Leave the Jensen behind for me to drive."

She gave him a mock punch. "No chance. That car is the key to my wandering spirit, it knows when and where to lead me."

CHAPTER SEVENTEEN

Emerging into bright sunshine from Siena's smart passenger building, Richie saw the magic metal blue of the Jensen before he picked out his mother. It was eighteen months since they had separated in her kitchen. She was full of smiles, her hair long enough to reach the hem of a yellow flowery dress which was short enough to show lots of tanned leg. He was apprehensive, having jacked in his job at the canning factory, and after some drifting and stalling, taken the plunge to travel to Tuscany. It had been a long journey, by various coaches and trains, with spasmodic meals, to reach her.

On the trip he'd had ample time to think and he read her many letters over and over again. Postmarks from Paris, several towns in Spain, the south of France and Geneva charted her nomadic voyage that had stopped here about a year ago. He was searching for something in her footsteps that he needed to lead him to the new person he was anxious to be.

With his head rumbling on big glass windows, much of Europe had flashed by while his mind was full of the natural creature mother had become. There were many references to friendships quickly forged, brave adventures leading to bruises and blemishes, and decisions made with the heart. She followed the stars, she told him, to wherever they might lead. The open eternity of the universe was her inspiration.

She'd occasionally include a photo, taken with some misty Polaroid. One showed her knees poking through ripped jeans, another, her lying on the floor of someone's lounge smoking a cigar. All had the same ever present smile. In his favourite, she stood at the top of a bell tower with the lights of some town sparkling beneath her like a thousand diamonds.

He wondered if he had that kind of courage, to throw himself at life and not dwell on the past. Was she fooling herself, and therefore him? He had grown up with a father who controlled the future with certainty, confident his plans would lead to wealth and through that wealth find freedom. Richie had

119

admired that approach until he began to doubt the kind of rewards it would surely bring. His mum highlighted a different way. He had to embrace her love of uncertainty, revel in the moment when simple pleasure brought joy, if he was going to make it work for himself. He was ready to try.

His mother was triumphant. She soared towards him with arms outstretched.

"Wonderful, wonderful!" she shouted, making him drop his suitcase to receive the love.

Once she had spun them around and pressed her cheek to his, she stood before him, holding each of his arms as if he might blow away. He was unshaven, dishevelled, perhaps a little thinner.

"I can't believe you are here. I have so much to show you!"

His face had flushed and he watched passersby to see if this extravagant hello was deemed worthy of attention. It appeared not. Public demonstrations of affection were likely the norm.

"It's good to be here, mum. Though I confess it was a long journey. I'm sure it will be worth it."

"Come on, let's get going."

The car was close by. He never got tired of seeing its sleek lines and big wheels. Round the back, above the two powerful exhaust pipes and the chrome bumper, his stuff disappeared down into a sizeable boot.

"Glad to see the Jensen has survived, still in good condition," he remarked.

"My pride and joy," she said.

When they took off, he gripped the handle in the door while she dodged and weaved through disorderly traffic. He found himself glancing out of all the windows. They appeared to be surrounded. The teddy bear was unmoved on the back seat, or perhaps frozen by fear?

"You have to drive like them to avoid them," she explained, chuckling.

His first impression of the place, as they climbed the hill towards the main centre, was of very old, rustic buildings worn at the edges by time and a dusty climate. Some local people appeared to be in a similar state, while others were elegant to a showy degree. Smart boutiques mingled with market stalls and on one corner, goats were tethered, sitting comfortably on the ramshackle pavement.

Into an incredibly compact area was fitted some fine, large buildings housing government, the opera, a museum and a hotel. Topping all of these, and indeed the entire area, were towers. One, the cathedral, sat in perfect magnificence, white marble patterned with black, stretching up with the number of windows increasing by one at each level. It felt like every available penny had been spent on this house of worship, leaving the surrounding area to shabbiness.

His mother crouched low to share in his view. "Very regal, isn't it. Too many idols, too much trumped up pomp. Let the devil take them! I prefer the quaint and the tumbledown. Just as well!"

As if to demonstrate her observation, she turned manically to the left down a street so narrow it must have been laid out in medieval times. Even the Jensen struggled to remain dignified on these cobbles, shaking and shuddering in disapproval.

He glanced at his mother. She was smiling, showing no alarm at how close the door of each dwelling was to the wings of her car. Just when he thought he'd experienced the tightest squeeze she went down through an arch so constricted he shut his eyes. Hearing no crunch of metal he opened them again to find they were in a mini square with no other exit. His quizzical expression made her laugh.

"I live here," she explained. "Jump out, I'll show you."

He did just that, still shaking a bit from the drive. He was confronted on each side by stone and brick in various shades of red and brown. Above where they had come in, a thin tower topped by russet coloured tiles accommodated two old iron bells connected to a rope that stretched down out of sight. Attached at a lower level was a wooden scaffold covered with

121

vines. Directly before them was a bar called Sirena advertising strong coffee and aperitifs.

He breathed deeply the warm, sandy odour and shook his head to reset his senses. A whole jumble of life co-existed in this one little area. And his mother was in the middle of it.

"Come," she urged, taking his hand. "We'll come back down for your things in a minute."

She led him through the bar. It was shadowy inside, lit by lamps that seemed as yellow as the walls. There were many dark tables but only a few customers, all rather sleepy or reflective. A tall chap with much brown hair, sideburns and a wide moustache, was operating a coffee machine. He stopped and his face lit up. He said something in Italian with much enthusiasm.

"Thank you," his mother replied. "This is my son," she added, proudly. The man looked very pleased and came out from behind his counter to shake hands. Richie was surprised by the firmness of his grip and the roughness of his skin.

"Surely, Carol. You are not old enough!" he cried. His voice was strong and loud.

"I'm afraid so," she said.

"Ah, never too much," he countered. "Don't forget, you owe me that dance. Later, perhaps?"

"Soon."

He stepped up close to her, bent down and whispered something into her ear. She sniggered and fell into his bulky frame at which point Richie noticed he had his considerable palm planted on his mother's behind, up under her dress.

"Enough, see to your customers," she insisted, pushing him playfully away. "Rich, let's go."

They went up some predictably narrow wooden stairs to a door that she produced a key for. With a small shove, they were inside and he saw for the first time the room she had described in her letters.

It was cluttered but only by charm and character. There were lots of diminutive tables, covered by flowers or papers or intricate ornaments and lamps. Many pictures and paintings of green landscapes covered the plain, grey walls, above which a lavish border of swirling leaves in ochre and white added drama. A big, blue, velvet sofa took up the most space, lit by frosted windows. Framed by rich claret curtains, a door made of rich oak inset with chequered, multi coloured glass, led to on to the bedroom.

"Amazing," Richie said.

"Suits me. Quiet considering how near the city centre is. It was a writer's place for years. He died a while back. Most of this stuff was his."

"Was he famous?"

"Not at all, I don't think. Promising I think they described him as. Then again, the world is full of novelists who would be fabulous if someone noticed."

"I like it."

"So sit, let's have a drink to celebrate your coming."

As he sank into the large seat, she threw the windows open with a flourish. The vast expanse of sky and a complete lack of traffic noise made it seem very unlike a city. Somewhere in the distance a lonely bell was sounding. She came back from the fridge with a bottle. When she leant over the coffee table to fill their glasses, her dress gaped and revealed to Richie more than he would ever have wished for. He looked away quickly with embarrassment flushing through his blood.

It was clear that she had become even freer than before. This bra-less, hippy woman, readily flashing flesh and smiles was a long way from the retiring mother of his youth. He would not have recognised her if not for the familiar lines of her collar bone and arching eyebrows.

"How do you afford to live like this?" he asked, as she lounged beside him.

"You told me dad's money was getting thin before you left."

"I work a bit in the bar downstairs. Plus I stay here rent free courtesy of the guy who owns it now."

"That's generous!"

"Kind of," she said, with a pout. "He gets the odd favour from me so I guess he gets a kind of payment."

"Mother!" Richie reacted, appalled at this information and her readiness to share it.

"What the hell! You're old enough now. The world knows the worth of a woman's charms."

"You taught me my morals. I remember you saying I would be protected by the rules if I kept to them."

"Oh stop looking so serious and disappointed. It's who I am now. I've not fallen as far from grace as you think. You set me too high to start with."

"So you think it's a wise way to act."

She put her glass on the table with a clunk. "Listen. You should know something. I have a lover too. He's never going to leave his wife and family, we both know the score. An Italian man sees a mistress as essential as a car."

Richie put his head into his hands. "My god," he groaned. "You're nearly fifty and....and....your my mum."

"Come on, it's no big deal. I like the attention and the things he buys me but he could come or go tomorrow and I wouldn't be much affected."

He looked at her now, his jaw tight, while he tried to arrange his thoughts.

She pushed her hair out from her neck, spraying it in a fan. "Give us a smile. I'm happy. Be glad for me."

"The hardest thing about all this is how casual you are. So much pure abandon. I can't get how you can be so chilled."

"Put it down to experience."

124

"I suppose," Richie said. "It still feels weird. I mean, aren't parents supposed to do all this before their kids are born?"

"The world is changing, Richie."

"Right. I must try and understand that. Maybe the best is still to come for me."

Carol nudged his elbow with hers. "Believe me, after you've been dished some real dirt most things taste sweet."

He took a very large gulp of wine and hoped she was right.

CHAPTER EIGHTEEN

Richie awoke to strange scents in the complete darkness. It took his mind a moment to move out of his dream where the devil disguised as a magician was trying to trick him into giving up his soul. Now where was he?

With a jerk, he sat up and swung his feet off the bed onto cold tiles. This was Italy, his mother's apartment; he had taken an afternoon nap to ease his aching head. The slightest hint of light bled through in a vertical line before him. He located the latch for the shutters and threw them open. A gorgeous pink sky glowed beyond, forcing the cathedral to blush at the beauty that surpassed it. All the surrounding rooftops looked soft, covering harder lives and gloomy stories with rustic charm.

He marvelled at the scene until he shut his eyes in hope that he might retain the image forever. Then he moved into the next room to find his mother before an easel capturing the very same loveliness more effectively on canvas.

"When did you get to be any good at art?"

She smiled at his begrudged compliment. Her much worn apron spoke of many hours spent practicing. "Time on your own teaches you. And there was a guy I met in Dijon who gave me lessons. We'd drive out in the Jensen and paint the most amazing landscapes and then make love to celebrate our art."

Richie was keen to avoid hearing too much more about that. "Can you show me? I'd like to give it a try."

Carol was pleased. "Of course. The more we can share the better. How was your sleep?"

He frowned. "Deep. And weird."

"That's the exhaustion of travelling so far and such quick time. Do you feel refreshed enough for me to introduce you to Siena by night."

"Why not? I came here to experience as much as possible."

126

He ran both hands through his floppy hair and prepared himself for the next phase of his initiation.

"I brought your suitcase up."

"On your own?" he queried, remembering the number of little steps they'd climbed.

"Yes."

"It's well heavy."

"I'm not some weedy housewife, you know. Do you think I'd have gotten this far without being strong? Now go and shower and put on your best stuff. You can be the man tonight."

~

Arm in arm they went across cobbles and little squares. The evening was warm, the air sweeter than during the day, and Richie liked it. At a table on the pavement beneath a faded red, green and white striped awning they drank Campari as she described her way of life now.

"I don't waste time anymore," she said. "All that worrying whether I was doing the right thing or if anyone was unwell and the fear of getting old too soon. I think I was angry about how much I gave to the family and how little I got for me.

"I bruise just the same I guess, but I don't feel it like I did. The flame I sparked off inside me the day I bought that car has lit the way and brought eternal warmth. Those headlights led me to a point where I knew I could do whatever I wanted. I've driven through the turning tide in the moonlight, naked from the waist up. That Jensen made it to a little chapel on a steep mountainside and raced with the pride of German youth on the autobahn in the Black Forest."

"I'm glad you've had such happiness."

She leaned down to catch his eyes with hers. "Except?"

"I mean it," he assured her.

127

"There's doubt in your voice. I haven't seen much of you lately but I know when you're hiding something."

"Well, this is all so odd and confusing. I've tried to get used to it. Each time I get reconciled in my head you seem to go a step further into the wild."

Carol sat back and laughed. "There's too much of the conventional in you. It's partly my fault. I brought you up that way. Then I had to change and you couldn't."

He felt crestfallen. A group of young people breezed past, boys and girls entwined physically and mentally, as carefree as his mother.

"I guess there's hope for me, I am your son after all. If you pulled this off, so can I. It must be in my blood!"

"What was good for me may not be right for you."

He became even graver, the yellow of the streetlamps carving sharp lines on his face. "I suppose that is what worries me most."

"You'll need to find your own way."

"I can't, don't you see!"

His intensity took her by surprise. She listened very carefully while he recalled with considerable emotion the restlessness of his university years.

"I don't know what to believe in because there's nothing I trust. I've grown to realise I'm not at one with myself or the world around me.

"You offered hope. I'd imagine your adventures, spiced up by the odd postcard and letter I got. You travelled underneath the great stars, out where the sea foams, the wind making music in your long hair. I gazed up from within your shadow and worried about how much your lovers might rob or when you might fall from grace and be strewn like dirt on the stony ground, taking all my hopes with you."

Now she bit her finger to stifle a tear. "I had no idea...."

He smiled apologetically. "No pressure."

"And I thought you idolised your father."

128

"I did, until you became the unlikely heroine, all whimsical like castles in the air."

"You make it sound so poetic."

"I did study literature at Uni," he reminded her. "Much to dad's consternation."

"And what of Marcus, how is he? You haven't mentioned him until now."

"I didn't think you liked talking about him."

She waved her hand dismissively, the romantic red paint still visible on her knuckles. "Oh, that was before. It's much easier now. I'm completely over him."

"He's the same as ever. Very wrapped up in business. He sent his regards but warned me to be careful not to let you lead me astray."

"Then astray you must go!" she concluded, her wink in tune with her mischievous manner.

~

They drank aplenty that night, visiting various establishments where Carol always seemed to be known to someone, usually male. As he watched Siena society, he decided it was a domain where men reigned. Heads of families, first born sons, bar owners, all filled with confidence as they flirted with women and were attended to by dutiful wives and girlfriends.

Then, when he watched his mother, with her easy smile and uninhibited actions, he changed his mind. This was a city of opportunity for the free spirited, the ones prepared to live and love to the full and not fret over the consequences. The total opposite of what he was used to in the north of England.

The buildings crumbled, weeds grew through uneven pavements, the paint on the walls flaked. And yet, in the darker cafes, people like his mother found glory in the candlelight, a mature woman in full bloom, her sparkling jewels drawing glances and attention from all who saw her. She sought delight, found it, revelled in it, and flew with it until all the hours of night were

129

gone and they returned to her apartment to watch the sun come up over a mist with their drowsy eyes.

~

It wasn't the only time in those first few weeks that they came home exhausted. Whether by night or day, she had so much to show him that they stopped only to eat long and luxuriously or to sleep. She manoeuvred the big Jensen with ease through the narrow streets and their ragtag of daily life, always knowing secret places to park.

He took in the obvious architectural highlights and some immense museums. There was much of great antiquity. Inside the St. Dominic Basilica she took particular amusement in his reaction to the dismembered head of St. Catherine, enshrined in gold and revered as a relic. He stared with bizarre fascination at the yellow skin and deathly expression.

"That's sick!" he complained, once they were back outside.

"It's very serious for some people, she had visions of Jesus, suffered greatly in her devotion. She's revered."

"There's no self-respect. Pretending stuff like that can have an effect on us. I've gone cold."

She leaned into him to offer comfort as they strolled slowly away. "Not your thing? Don't you want a piece of me to keep once I've gone?"

"No. I love you but you need dignity in death."

"I don't think you're going to find any answers there then," she concluded, bringing them to a stop beside a stone facade held up by many pillars and topped by a flag. "Want something more modern? A friend of mine has a gallery here, lots of contemporary paintings."

He found a grin for his pale face. "Yes, that's sounds better."

Within, it was cool and very quiet. Paintings of assorted size covered the large white walls. There didn't seem to be any theme or pattern. What they had in common was boldness and bright colours.

130

He was aware she had seen all of them several times before and was more intent to wait for his responses. When he failed to register any great joy she became unsettled. The finger chewing had started again.

"Do you not like anything you see?" she asked after developing a large frown.

"I'm not sure," he replied, sounding more confused than bored.

"What about this one? What do you see?"

"A track, through some woodland."

"I know that!" she said with a growl. "How does it make you feel?"

"Afraid. I don't know what is in those shadows."

She looked at him with disbelief. "I count it as a favourite. The use of light, the sense of mystery. You can imagine birds flitting in the branches and sense the leaves trembling in the breeze."

He went to move on. She held her arm out to prevent him.

"Don't you want to take that path and see what you might find?"

"No," he said, firmly.

"I think there's a sweet voice singing somewhere deep within the trees, calling me."

He shook his head and she let him continue. Each subsequent picture produced only more melancholy.

"Bringing you in here was a mistake," she surmised. "I don't think galleries are for you any more than dead heads."

"No mum," he countered. "If you like them I want to share. I need to understand what it means to you."

She leaned against the wall while contemplated the next offering, and gazed towards the high ceiling, recalling a special memory.

"It was on my first trip in the Jensen, when I went to a place like this, and found fantastic expression through the colours. The rich ones, crimsons and coppers, are the best."

"There's too much pain on show. And all the angles and lines are sharp, cutting and hurting."

"Emotion revealed is like the ocean unfurled," she stated.

"Complete with storms," he added.

"No wonder you struggled when we spent that day teaching you the basics of art."

She took each of his hands and stared up at him, the lines showing on her face under the bright gallery lights.

"I'm worried about you. There must be one painting here you find appealing?"

"There was one," he said, and then grimaced. "Or maybe not."

"Show me!"

He was reluctant.

"Oh, come on!" she pleaded. "You must share with me otherwise I'll never know you any better."

He shrugged and took her back to the picture that had stirred him. It was of a girl in an erotic pose, full of dark allure and suggestion. While Richie blushed, Carol grinned shrewdly.

"Well that's telling," she declared. "It is time we set you loose."

CHAPTER NINETEEN

"Nothing is any clearer," Richie said, looking straight out over the Jensen's expansive bonnet as late afternoon Siena parted at his mother's twist of the wheel. "Do I have to be patient?"

"How would I know?" she replied, shrugging her bare, bony shoulders.

"Because you seem to know how to live."

"Beware idolising me. I've warned you about that before."

She glanced at his stoic face. It's brooding was enough to cast a cloud across the beautiful golden sunlight that stole through the narrow streets.

"Oh, Richie. Why so serious? You might find happiness if you made the most of the here and now. You've just finished work, we have money, a fast car, the night beckons and there no deadlines to meet."

"I think I'm weighed down by it all."

"Well that's not good."

"Perhaps it is."

She dismissed his malaise with an unsympathetic smile and an increase in speed. His spirits sank with him into the loud red seat. Whenever he moaned like this he felt worse. He made his own problems and each time the solution he reached for failed, his options narrowed.

He thought back over the months since his arrival. All those fine restaurants and the new food he had tried. The big gathering his mother had arranged at her apartment where an eclectic mix of people had offered their insight; drink and drugs were passed around like candy at a kid's birthday; women laid out an incorrigible path to wickedness which he willingly took to many drink fuelled encounters. The job he started at the bar brought another new experience. Easy money so quickly spent. And still the anticipated rise above the ordinary eluded him. He had no purpose and he felt he needed it.

"Look, if you don't cheer up I'll leave you behind tonight," Carol said when she stopped the car in their little square. "Your problem is," she continued,

133

winding up her window to keep their heated dialogue unheard. "You are becoming old too soon. I made the same mistake, getting serious with your father. I lost the love of life."

"And had me."

"Which was wonderful. But you have no commitments. Just enjoy yourself, like I do."

"It doesn't work for me."

"Then you might as well go home."

"Good, I'm weary with all the 'fun'."

He made a sarcastic gesture of jazz hands which made her tighten her fingers into claws. "I've set you up the best I can. Michele employed you on my persuasion, and you've met everyone I believe worthy."

"And so I should just be grateful and happy?"

"At least try."

"Well I can't. Pretending is not my speciality."

"So you being miserable is my fault?"

"Yes," he affirmed.

Her stare burned into the side of his head for what she considered long enough to garnish a reaction. When none was forthcoming she snarled and got out with a flourish. It was a little while before he joined her in the apartment. She was cooking eggs in the kitchen, the oil crackling like the tension in the air. After he had stretched out on the big blue sofa she came in and threw down the food onto the dining table with a clatter.

"A meal for his lordship," she announced with a bitter hiss.

He came to the table like a naughty four year old and mumbled his gratitude. After watching him eat for a while she could hold on to her frustration no longer.

"I didn't ask you to come here. You never gave it a second thought, so sure I was that goddess you sought to worship and follow. And now you feel short changed and I have to take the blame. That's not fair."

He would not meet her eye. "I realise that," he admitted.

"So what do you intend to do next?"

"Don't know." His head dropped.

"How about a good cry? Or the opposite!? Whatever....just stop making such a big deal and being so self important."

He went on chewing but his senses were numb. No flavour or smell reached him, his body was listless.

She leaned forward to try and see his face. "Look, I've had my share of anguish. I know what anger feels like. Whether it was since I left and when I was married, I kept going. There's not much more you can do."

He put down his cutlery and looked at his mother's radiance, bright despite the passage of the years, and his stomach knotted. It was the destiny of every generation to be hamstrung by the previous one, whatever their intentions.

"You didn't make me ready for life," he said. "I got all of your insecurities piled on me like a heap of garbage. And when you decided you'd had enough, you fled."

"That's—"

"Let me finish," he commanded. "Now I took on the pressure, endeavoured to reach my father's expectations. Not much chance of that. So now I'm having a go at emulating my mother, only she created an environment of safety for me to grow up in and I can't cope with the wild and the free she has decided to embrace.

"I am the product of the both of you. I understand it isn't easy. So I don't truly hold you responsible. You just fucked up like any human would at such an impossible job. I was your safety net while you flew on the trapeze above. I'm as flat as the ground."

A silence followed this profound judgment. Carol pushed her own food around the plate while the sound of the deathly bells stole in through the open windows from the square. After some melancholic thought, she drew in a lungful of the warm air.

"I did what I could," she concluded.

He nodded slowly in agreement and they shared a shrug.

"Well," she said, becoming brighter in characteristically quick time. "My way, your father's way. Neither worked. So you need to find Richie's way."

"I guess," he agreed, without conviction.

"Meantime, I have a date with my own life's purpose. The city awaits."

He watched her flounce before the huge mirror while she decided if she needed to change before she went out. Her hair spun as she swung her head, flashing a wide smile and an expression of optimism. And yet again he was left wondering where he might find the same kind of elation.

~

It was a beautiful drive to Monteriggioni, past vineyards laden with grapes ready for harvesting. The summer was fading into a dusty brown. The timeless calm could not be ruffled even by the busy season ahead. An ancient fortress with fourteen towers, the little town commanded a neat hillside. From the walls the view to be absorbed was fantastic, yet Carol was quietly reflective as she planted her elbows on the stone.

"It is time for me to go back to England," she informed him.

Richie was confused. The breeze blew his unruly hair while he chewed this over. He reached no conclusions. "I don't understand. You love it here."

"I'm getting too old. Just lately I've been feeling so tired. I need the care and comfort of home."

"Are you sure?"

She twisted and leaned against the battlements, her body still thin and supple. "Oh, believe me, I've thought about it lots. It makes me sad but I have to be realistic. My adventure has to continue somewhere else."

"How soon?"

"In a few weeks. I don't want to dally."

136

It was Richie turn to gaze out over the patchwork of rural Italy and wonder what place it had for him.

"Will you go back slowly? Take a year to get there?"

"I'm flying," she said.

Richie started several sentences but got no further than the first word each time.

"Oh, poor Richie. I need to be more honest with you. Truth is, I'm unwell. All the signs point to cancer. I'm going home to sort it out. I still qualify as an English citizen."

"I'll come with you," he responded, without hesitation.

"No. I want you to stay here. You've taken a year to adjust, you need to keep going."

He gripped his mother's bony arms. "You'll need me to take care of you. It's my place, beside you."

"It's all arranged. I'm going to stay with Lori, she has a huge house she rattles around in since her children grew up and her husband went off with that dancer."

"I thought you'd fallen out with her? She didn't like you finding freedom, you said."

Carol smiled. "She discovered the hard way that there is more to life than money and expensive home furnishings. She came out here for a few weeks last year; we had a whale of a time. It was like we were as we left school, just looking for laughs."

"How can I carry on when—"

She planted her palm over his mouth. "I won't hear any more, let's go and get some lunch, I'm starving."

~

They did not mention her imminent departure again until after the meal. Richie drank some of the excellent local wine and was soothed. The world bustled by across the neatly patterned stones of Piazza Roma, the medieval towers cast their shadows and time came to a brief halt. When they stretched back in the ornate metal chairs to sip the small, strong coffee, the moment was right for them to return to her ill-fated news.

The noises of the town faded into a quiet that existed exclusively between them.

"I'll leave you the car," she said.

"Your dream?"

She looked up into the pure blue sky. "It changed me for sure but it can't save me."

"I can drive back–"

"If and when I'm ready, I'll tell you."

"You might return."

"I don't think so. If I travel again I'll seek somewhere new."

Richie's anxiety was growing rapidly. It was as if she had already gone; the turmoil boiled. He fiddled with the edge of the tablecloth. "I haven't got a hope without you around."

"That's nonsense! I'll make sure you can stay on in the apartment."

"How, when you won't be able offer a personal payment of the rent?"

"Oh, I think I've built up enough credit for a year or two. That should get you to a point when you can make some choices."

Richie sighed. "This is all so bloody final, like you've worked it through to a conclusion."

"I have to face what is coming. And I believe you will be okay."

"Me? Alone? I don't think so."

"You aren't alone. My friends are yours."

"Your world will be out of my reach."

Carol punched her chin in frustration. "You have Alessia now. She's a real cracker."

"It's very new. I'm not even sure she likes me that much. She's your friend's daughter, she's likely seeing me to please her mum."

"Always so negative," Carol grumbled.

Richie sat up in his defence. "Well I'll tell you something positive. You are my anchor, you give me gravity. I'm afraid I'll drift off without you."

"I'm an anchor? That's a bad joke. Maybe ten years ago, not anymore."

He got up abruptly and walked away. She threw her hands up then dropped them onto her head. Hurriedly finding her purse, she threw money onto the table and went after him. His path was predictable. He returned to the car and she found him leaning on the boot with hands in pockets, staring at the ground.

She got in without speaking and a forceful rev of the engine brought him scrambling in beside her. They did not speak until Siena was visible on the hilly horizon.

"Just think, this beautiful motor will be yours," she said. "But I'm taking the bear!"

He wasn't impressed but he did glance around the expansive cockpit. He imagined himself at the wheel, sweeping around gritty corners, climbing and falling through the Tuscan landscape. Then he shook the image from his brain.

"You expect me to live some kind of carefree, bohemian life here while you are far away going through treatment for cancer."

"Yes, Richie, I do. You won't be able to do anything there except fret. I'll be happier knowing you are building on what you have. If I get really bad, then you can come and sit with me, read me that poetry you love."

"And if I make a mess of things in Italy? What then?"

"You won't. Your time has come. With all you've got, and good looks as well, this place is made for you."

They went over a crest and the road snaked ahead through a green valley before them. The dropping sun burned orange, setting the tips of leaves on fire, and to Carol it was a beautiful painting in the making. Richie saw the steep hill on the other side.

CHAPTER TWENTY

There was a girl sitting up at the window, in a lacy black bra and black mini skirt, her cigarette smoking fading into the cityscape beyond. He drifted in and out of consciousness but she remained there, her back to him, rich dark hair tumbling onto her shoulders. She merged with a dream he was having until he wasn't sure what part was real.

When the bells began ringing in the church beside the little square, he was roused sufficiently to sit up. She turned her head and her velvety gaze fixed on him, one eyebrow arched quizzically. Here was a vision, the promise of eternal summer, a deep forbidden wish. She was beautiful.

He wanted her to come and relieve his aching brow with her smooth fingers, help him understand where he was, who he was. Instead, she stayed put, maintaining an eerie silence.

Now his brain began to try and function. There was a fuzzy recollection of the night before. They were tumbling across the sofa together, she was laughing deliciously. He watched her do an impromptu dance, both twee and suggestive, teasing him from across the room. When he tried to get up he fell across the coffee table, sending pills and white powder everywhere. Then her face had changed, she was shaking him and shouting.

He flopped back onto the bed and listened to her breathing, or was it sighing? When he looked her way again she was gone. The sky was very blue outside and the sounds of people going about their business bounced around the old buildings. With a stumble he made it to the mirror, where he found a note from the angel. Even her handwriting was elegant.

"Gone to be with the living."

"Shit!" he groaned, before sinking into a heap on the floor.

~

Later, much later, he went out to look for her. First, he had to recover, recoil, regret, regroup, reassess. It was a slow process. He shuffled around

140

the apartment, half hoping to see his mother's smile and get her help clearing up the place.

But he was alone. He had let himself slip into this cheerless spinning routine of a dope on dope, a drunk on drink. A short release then the long lock-in of soulless darkness.

Alessia kept him going. He needed her. She could save him. She was the good part of this life, so far ahead of him. He had to keep touch with her so she could drag him out of the mess. With his mother so far away, Alessia was the one to show the way.

Once he had tidied, he sat in the big blue sofa and looked out on the rain that fell in sheets now, dripping steadily from the open shutters. All else was quiet. The record he had put on to boost the mood had long since finished. He was afraid. Without Alessia his last source of pleasure would be gone. He roused himself from this trance with a shake of his head. Outside, the clouds had rolled on and the sun was bright again on the terracotta roofs. How long had he been there? His neck was very stiff. He went and had a shower, that started very hot and ran through to cold, reviving his weary limbs. In best clothes, with his droopy hair neatly combed, he went out to the Jensen.

Up at the wheel, he surveyed this great power machine and some of his pride returned. He knew people noticed him when he drove around Siena. How could such a young kid own such a beast? He must be *somebody*. Then the doubts came crawling back, up through the rumbling engine, snatching at his arms and pressing him down into the big seat. Was it the car that Alessia loved, not him? She was always describing the rush she felt when he accelerated.

He pulled off in a hurry, keen to leave any daemons behind. He stopped at the flower stall his mum always frequented and bought a single red rose, setting it carefully onto the passenger seat while he continued on to where Alessia lived.

Her mother answered the door. She had an older version of her daughter's dusky looks and used her arching eyebrows to an equally devastating effect. Richie thought his will was going to shatter like fine crystal.

"She hasn't heard a thing from you in two days," she stated, her words enough to damn him.

"I....wanted....to....be....in the right place....before I came round," he stuttered, without conviction. His use of his own language had been inferior to hers.

To his relief, she held the door wide open. "I don't think much of her taste in men. She's by the pool, don't expect a warm welcome."

He went through and as he approached her, he lingered in the shadows within. She was lying out on her front wearing only the smallest of bikini bottoms. Her skin was bronzed, sparkling in the sunlight from a recent swim, and the contours of her body dipped and curved in perfection. With a gulp, he walked slowly towards her, like a barely believing fan approaching a lifelong idol.

"Hi, baby," he said, trying to sound casual but failing as his voice cracked. She lifted herself onto her elbows but did not turn to look his way. Instead, she seemed to be contemplating the easy ripples on the blue water.

"How are you?" he asked, lamely.

Still, she did not answer.

"Nice hot afternoon."

Finally, she relented. "Leave me alone, I don't want to be disturbed."

To hear her voice was thrilling. She spoke good English thanks to her father coming from London. It had a delicious Italian accent that reminded him of Sophia Loren.

He placed the flower beside her. "I wanted to apologise."

"I wanted to make you disappear."

He was flummoxed. He put his arms out wide, dropped them again, pushed them into his pockets and ran the soles of his shoes over the patio.

142

"What can I do to make it right?"

"Go away."

"Okay, then."

As he turned to go, she threw him the lifeline of further conversation.

"I'm fed up. You went too far again, after you said you wouldn't. You do too much bad stuff. You make me angry. You're gonna kill yourself and it isn't easy to watch. I won't stand around while you destroy everything. So I walk away."

"I'm so sorry!" he cried and instinctively crouched down to stroke her shoulder.

When his touch was not repelled he turned it into a caress, tracing a line down to the small of her back. Her skin was like velvet.

"I've been thinking. I'm gonna throw away all those bad habits. I've blown my mind so many times. Now I've collected all the pieces together and I'm whole again."

He waited for her response with baited breath, all the while marvelling at her incredible shape. A suggestive wiggle of her backside invited his fingertips to explore lower. As he enjoyed her response, she turned to face him at last, with a broad smile and naked breasts. She picked up the rose and breathed in the scent with great gusto. Her incredible features lit up in appreciation.

Her dark eyelashes fluttered while she took a moment to think. "We'll take the car out of Siena," she concluded. "Go up into the hills to a place I know. It is lovely there."

Richie grinned too. In the arms of this magical seductress there was salvation for fools like him.

~

Alessia came along quickly, dancing out of her door pulling a short, summery white dress over her head. Richie revved the engine and she

143

laughed. The last thing they saw as they roared away was her mother's head shaking at the window.

"She doesn't like me," he said.

"What has she seen to like? You turn up when you can be bothered, leave me sad. She had to come and rescue me from that vineyard you stranded me at. You're English, the same as the man who left her. And you never smile when you come round, she thinks you lack sparkle. I've lost track of the number of times she's asked me if you were adopted. She loved your mum's energy and sense of fun."

"Nothing much going for me then?" he commented dryly.

"You might just try with her a bit."

"She scares me," he said, with a shudder. "I'll show her yet."

"Well, good," Alessia encouraged. "Coz I know your qualities. She just needs that showing."

She patted his leg and the effect was electric. Of the few girls he'd been with, she was the only one who could make his heart pound like it was now. As they reached the edge of the city and white stone gave way to greens and yellows, he pushed his right foot down to bring the Jensen into its own. He passed two cars, a tractor and man on a donkey, with suicidal speed, leaving a cloud of dust in their wake.

"Favoloso!" Alessia cried, waving a brown arm out of the window.

When the car was running fast, Richie felt released from the burdens that hunted him. He could outrun anything and with Alessia delirious beside him, they were united.

"What's this dent in the dash here?" she enquired, tracing a line with her bare toes.

"Don't know. Mum told me it was there when she bought it."

"Something hit here with a big bump."

144

"I'm sure it was nothing. This car has magic. The power to renew life. Mum's proof of that. Who could drive this machine and not have every kind of luck come their way!"

She seemed about to argue against this logic, but instead she pointed to the right. "Turn there," she directed.

With a broad sweep, he came off the main route and dipped into the shadow of the hills ahead.

"Wow, this is a rough road, even by local standards," he observed.

"We always came here for picnics when I was a girl, before daddy got miserable and left."

She had rarely mentioned her father, hiding him away with a perfunctory wave and quick change of subject whenever the topic came up. Richie nearly sought more information with a question but a brief glance at her told him she was lost in bittersweet memories. They came to a point where the track split in two, she indicated left, up above the tree line where the land dipped down again, bringing them to a small ridge overlooking the way they had come.

They both got out to contemplate the view. The effect was lessened by low cloud that had returned to empty its load for a second time that day. It amounted to nothing more than a light drizzle on the humid air. They shared a bottle of cola while they leaned against the warm bonnet.

"I'm impressed," she smiled. "No drinking tonight."

"I don't think I could face it after that last bender," he admitted. He examined the label. "This has plenty of sugar, it'll keep me going."

She dropped her head onto his shoulder, lots of sumptuous hair flowing down and across her face. "You see, when you get away from the city pressures, how simple it can be."

He put an arm around her. "So you came here with your dad?"

145

"Him, yes. And everybody. The family, grandpa and grandma, my cousins and uncles, Aunt Giorgia, friends. So many. They were happy days. I tried wine for the first time. Mum said I never stopped giggling."

"I bet you were funny."

"Most people say I was annoying. Silly kid."

They laughed lightly together.

"What about you?" she asked, bringing her dark eyes and expectant brows to bear on him. "Do you have memories like that?"

"A few. A trip to the zoo I recall, or the first time I went to the theatre in London. I use the good bits to make me smile but they don't stay strong for long enough. I mostly hate the falseness of childhood, the lies you get told about stuff working out if you do as your parents say. They had no more of a clue back then than I did."

She moved in front of him and put her fists on his chest. "And what are you doing now? Drifting as you are is no better. Some of the ideals they tried to show you are worth remembering, even if they didn't live up to them themselves."

"I can't work out what's best," he confessed.

"You can't blame them."

"I can," he said, looking away. "They could have got me ready for all this."

"No one can," she said, quite animated now. He had seen this formidable Italian fire before and he usually avoided it. "Life is too big for anyone to have all the answers. Your mother found happiness because she went out looking for it. She wasn't leading you to Utopia, this was her own trip. It's not her fault that you're without purpose. She's been gone nine months now, and what plan do you have?"

He shrugged. "She doesn't want me back until she's ready."

"What about you? What do you want to do?"

"Not sure....find a path?"

146

"Well, choose your path and put up with what you find," she said, with a dismissive wave.

"You're an expert now are you?"

"I've seen enough to have an opinion," she countered, forcing her shoulders back indignantly.

She was so beautiful, even in anger; he found it hard to argue.

The rage continued. "I've wasted enough days with you, hanging around, waiting for something to happen while you wrestle with your suffering. You want other people to solve your problems for you."

He folded his arms but had little other defence to offer. She was right and did not let up.

"And when you reach a dead end, you take all that stuff to shut out what you can't face. The actual thing you can't face is being unable to face things."

"You use drugs too!" he protested.

She pulled an expression surprisingly twisted for one with such flawless features.

"I smoke a bit of weed; it helps with a good time and makes the sex more intense. Except by then you're usually so paralytic I get nothing. So I please myself and leave you to crawl into your own hole."

"It's the only way I know. Since I was a boy, I've destroyed myself when I start to fail. My dad was a winner and then my mum went and did something incredible too. There was no space left for me to be anybody."

She moved closer, hugging him now. "We all share the same challenges. It's part of growing up, finding your own self."

"You did it well," he said. "You're terrific, you can be anyone you choose to be."

"So can you!"

He laughed and her frustration made her sink her teeth into his shoulder. Richie was roused by her energy, a lithe female body pressed against him in

147

a thin short dress. With a surge of passion he pushed his mouth against hers and sought her tongue between her cherry lips.

At first she tried to resist, thinking her fury was too intense to give in to desire. When his free hand found its way into her bikini bottoms and between her legs, the warmth in his fingers made her gasp. When they tumbled behind the car her the fight she had went from confrontation to lust. The urgency now was to remove clothes quickly enough for their sex to be as uninhibited as possible.

In the aftermath she held him as tightly as was possible but futility dominated. The weight of him on top of her was symbolic. With his heavy heart he would slip away again all too soon. Despite being young and liberated, making love in the open under a Tuscan moon, she felt old and weary with him. The sweat and issue of their passion ran into the dry dust beneath them and disappeared.

CHAPTER TWENTY ONE

For a week, the lovers lived the dream, both of them denying any doubts that underlay their fluffy relationship. Richie sensed her mistrust in the way she watched him but she actually gave only the kind attention he craved. She listened, coerced, caressed his brow when it furrowed and fuelled the fire of his ardour as the nymphet in fishnet stockings.

On the square beneath the apartment he pushed her back across the sleeping Jensen's boot and planted frenzied kisses on her neck. When he pulled down the zip of her dress she stopped him.

"Not here," she insisted.

"Why not, no one cares. This is Italy."

"I do. Let's go, we can carry on upstairs."

"You were happy enough a minute ago," he complained.

She pushed him off and he staggered into a heap on the cobbles.

"You've had too much to drink. You need to sober up a bit then we can do this properly."

"Fuck off. I'm fine," he said, getting to his feet and promptly falling down again.

She reassembled her clothing and stood with hands on hips, waiting for him. He frowned like he was trying to remember how he got to be there. Wasn't it just a moment since he had felt sure he could take on the world? Now he couldn't stand up. She walked over, her heels tapping harshly on the stone, retrieved the key from his pocket and went inside.

"I'll see you inside when you can make it."

~

He found her at the open shutters. She had watched him from above, a pile of loneliness sat in the harsh moonlight. The cool evening air was a relief to her after the musty bars of their revelry. She hoped his head had cleared as well as hers. He soon showed it had not.

"Get your clothes off then," he mumbled, walking into a table and sending the lamp crashing.

"You need to sleep," she replied, ignoring how he was overstepping the mark.

"I need something to drink," he countered and headed for the kitchen.

She intercepted him at the fridge. "No, you don't. Let's lie down for a while and when you wake up we can make love."

He pushed her aside and pulled out a new bottle of wine. "Cheap, German, goes down easy, unlike the Italians!"

When he got to the sofa, she was sitting there, upright, uptight.

"Hey, honey, have some with me, it'll loosen you up."

"No, thank you," she said.

"Suit yourself."

Richie drank without a glass, taking huge gulps and belching between each one.

"You have no manners," she commented.

"And you had such a special upbringing. Got all you ever wanted," he chimed, with an ironic tone. "Do they know their perfect little girl fucks like a train?"

She stood and prepared to leave, only to find he was following her.

"Go away. You're pissed. I'm off home."

"I'll walk you back," he said, falling into her so badly she had to hold him up.

As they were both brought lower by the dead weight of him, their faces went close.

"I'm sorry," he burbled. "It's just one night. I get carried away."

"You stink of drink," she said, coolly. "I don't want to be with you like this. Once the real Richie is back, call me."

As she guided him back into a chair, he began laughing uncontrollably.

"What's funny?" she demanded, in no mood for jokes.

"Me. I'm dead funny. The real Richie, he's a loser!"

She observed him for a moment, his red face, that stupid false happiness in his eyes and languid limbs he did not own, before picking up her bag and slamming the door on his irritating giggle.

He spoke to himself. "Well done, Richie, you're getting good at this."

He fell off the chair and his chuckling turned to gasping tears.

~

Richie revived again in time for the Palio di Siena, a traditional horse race in Piazza Del Campo, which Alessia loved. She held onto him tightly as they weaved their way through the throng of tourists, seemingly proud to have a handsome man on her arm. She cheered during the parade, when the blue colour of her contrade passed by, large flags waving.

"Nicchio, Nicchio!" she cheered.

Richie was less enamoured by events. His mother dragged him to one of these the previous year and he had grown tired of the noise and retreated to the apartment. But he was trying to be keener today, determined to be good company to Alessia. Her allegiance and passion were invigorating.

"Seashell, right?" he confirmed with her.

"Oh yes," she said. "We are a noble district, historically potters. We are very proud of our military history."

"It would be nice to feel part of something like that," he mused, watching the euphoria rising around him.

"You should. It is very exciting."

"When did Nicchio last win?"

"Three years ago. A wonderful day."

He could see the light of remembrance flash in her dark eyes and he got carried along by the electric atmosphere and Alessia's zeal. It led to the Piazza where a huge number of people were gathered, in surprisingly orderly fashion, for the start of the race. Ten horses ran the circle around the edge. As far as he could make out, through the blur of action, the dust and dirt,

151

Alessia's colours fell somewhere during the second lap of three. She was frustrated but continued to be enthralled by the spectacle of danger and thrills.

The intensity overwhelmed Richie. The pound of the hooves, the skidding and tumbling, so many flags aloft, such focus on one thing. And then it was over. All too briefly he had lost himself. As they sauntered through the dispersing crowd, he felt very deflated. He could get a longer fix than that.

~

The streets were clear the next morning when they drove out into a blazingly hot day. The Jensen had complained at first, struggling to start several times, but sounded rich and pleasing once Richie got the revs up.

"We should have lunch somewhere, sit in the shade, drink something long and cool," Alessia said, lying back on the red leather with her brown legs stretched out and toes wiggling.

"Mmm, good idea," he agreed. "I just need to pop in on a friend."

He stopped the car on a steep hill, leaving barely enough room for anyone else to get by.

"Won't be long," he said, opening the door.

"I'll come in with you."

"Err, I don't think you'll like this guy," Richie answered.

"We'll see."

He appeared round her side and rather than offering his hand he held it up in a defensive gesture.

"I'll be back in a minute," he insisted, and disappeared into a gap between the buildings.

Despite the affront, she waited patiently at first. There had been strong sincerity in Richie's affection last night and today she felt sexy and alive. When ten minutes became twenty her delicate fingers began to twitch, tapping on tanned thighs that felt the urge to move. The radio was not

152

enough to amuse her. A police car, siren blazing, rushed past, matching the pace of her pulse.

Leaping out, she went into the alleyway, rattled some doors and walked back and forth with mounting irritation. He could be in trouble or she might just be a stupid fool for hanging around. Either way, she was a mass of nerves, needing to do something.

So she climbed in to the driver's side and took his beloved motor away, steering carefully around the stone corners and raised pavements. Her uncle had given her a few lessons, enough to get her safely home.

Richie ran up soon after, steaming in the heat, panting, wild with anxiety. Seeing the Jensen safe outside the house he launched an attack on the front door, only for it to open before he could hit it.

Alessia stood defiant, nostrils flaring, breathing as noisily as he was. Their stares were matched, like two wrestlers about to start a bout.

"What were you thinking?" he exclaimed.

"I'll tell you what I was thinking. I'm hanging around for someone who doesn't care. He's not coming out. I'm an inconvenience to him who could be doing her own thing. So I left."

"I can't believe you'd do that?"

Richie strode up and down while she remained motionless in her self-assurance.

"You forgot about me."

"I did not! I just had a bit of....negotiating to do."

"So I could just sit there as the pretty bird in a cage. Well, I'm not that girl!"

He might have lashed out in frustration had he any such capability. Instead, he tried to make sense of it with the mind of a defeatist. He bit the skin of his forefinger.

"So I don't measure up to your expectations?" he asked.

"No. I want to be romanced as a lady should be, not abandoned! You're such a waster. What were you doing that was so important?"

153

"Nothing....much."

He turned away from her, only to find she grabbed him quickly, pulling him close.

"You can tell me?"

Her tone was coercive but her intentions were more devious. She reached into his trouser pocket and removed a small parcel, stepping back and holding it aloft like a prize.

"What have we here?" she wondered.

"Give it back," he pleaded, knowing she wouldn't.

She sniffed the white envelope and nodded with sad resignation.

"I thought so. And you said you'd given it up."

"I have," he claimed, only to change his words to, "I will."

"Really? I can see you're just going round in circles."

He rubbed his forehead, flopping his hair, and looked down at the ground.

"Richie, this stuff is going to make you crazy!

His reaction was just a shrug with an apologetic smile. For Alessia this was enough.

"I won't go crazy with you." She slapped his precious packet into his chest, pushing him back in the process. "Take your drugs and your fancy car and go away, as far as possible, from me. The sight of you disgusts me."

He staggered before correcting himself. The sun shone brightly into his face. "Alessia, no!" he begged. "I need you."

"I mean it. Don't call here again."

Her mother came out and stood behind her, creating an awesome double take of the same disdainful look. Facing this wall of resolution and his own sense of shame, he retreated without knowing which way to go.

~

At first he just drove, with eyes that saw but registered nothing. He missed the people watching him fly by, shaking their heads, and the sweet little girl sat on a wall playing the flute and kicking out her legs. The only thing he knew was distance. Get away from that scene at her house, lose the guilt and hopefully the bad parts of who he was. Facing a future without her was too much to bear. The dials in the cockpit swung high, the engine growled in anger. This vehicle could lead him through hell.

The roads went up, narrowed and twisted until he found himself at Alessia's favourite spot in the mountains. Had he come here on purpose? Was it to be closer to her? Here they had made furious love. This was a place of happiness. Special to that angel.

He got out and looked out on the rugged panorama, a beautiful stillness pervading the thick air all around. Like a perfect poem, with neat rhymes and sentiments expressed, he understood the simplicity. If life could only be this harmonious he wouldn't get so mixed up. That sky up there was so clear, pure and perpetual.

A bird was soaring effortlessly through the gleam of light. With a twist of tail, it could change direction, adapt to the sudden current if wind. He was captivated by the freedom and mastery on show as it surveyed the world underneath, dropping lower to see what Richie was. He could see enough to decide it was an eagle. What it made of him was unclear. It flew over his head and disappeared higher up the mountain.

He followed, pleased to have made this acquaintance with such a magical creature. The climb was not made easy by the great lumps of rock that time had thrown across the most level route. He became determined, enjoying once again the immediate high he got from having a purpose.

Over the ridge he saw the bird come down to ground. Assuming a low profile, Richie crawled across the ground separating them, ignoring scrapes to his knees and forearms. At a boulder he paused, knowing it was perched only feet above him. He attempted to slow his breathing enough to be quieter.

When he lifted his head over the top, a magnificent golden eagle stood before him. Quite why it did not fly off was a mystery. He felt it was just too

155

majestic, too commanding, for such a show of caution. Instead, it remained calm, returning his look with equal intensity, with a bright yellow eye centred with a black pupil.

It was a king, turning his attention to some hopeless usurper and after careful examination deciding to not be best pleased with him. Richie consciously shrank back. He was an intruder in its domain. Only those of pure blood were welcome here. His was soiled, running with poison, too easily abused.

He did not even register as a threat. It idly raised one foot and pecked at a claw. There was a measured assurance in the way it raised a wing to run its beak through the feathers. As there was going to be no more communication, one needed to withdraw. Richie was clear it should be him. He slid and shuffled away in haste. Once he had retreated sufficiently the great raptor rose, called imperiously to the gates at the end of the world and flew up out of sight.

Richie was left panting and euphoric. He lay there for an age, piecing together his emotions. He was honoured and blessed by this vision. He took a message from the beak of the champion. Go, and be free from impurity. Claim the dominion of your own existence. In less poetic terms, clean up you act, be yourself, and you'll get the girl back as well as making your parents proud.

He ran now, over the huge chunks of rock, leaping and landing with new found precision. There was an answer; he wanted to share his insight with those who mattered. He needed to use this wave of positivity because it was rare in him. Unfortunately, he hit an immediate and major problem. When he returned to the ridge, his car had gone.

CHAPTER TWENTY TWO

The Jensen Interceptor looked resplendent even though the February afternoon light was thin. Paintwork and chrome sparkled, as good as new. It threw a blue tone on the dark skin of the two suited men standing to attention, waiting for the boss to appear.

When he came out of the villa's decorated door, they waited in hope for his approval of their efforts at polishing. He was an important man to please. It showed in his gait, a rolling swagger that was probably the only way he could walk having such a rotund frame. With thick eyebrows that threatened trouble and shaded his small and mean eyes, he was the kind of person you had to respect. The curly hair, cut short with precision, made his head appear big. In fact, his face seemed to swell the closer it got to his flabby neck. Not that anyone laughed at him. It was best to only react if he spoke to you.

He, like his employees, was smart in a fine brown striped jacket and black trousers. His highly polished leather shoes crunched crisply on the gravel drive, adding to the tension that persevered as he went around the vehicle slowly, taking in the detail. Once he had opened the driver's door and sat in, he took a firm hold of the steering wheel and nodded.

"Excellent, gentlemen," he said, in the Italian he preferred over his native Gheg.

"All the paperwork checks out now," Plator, the senior of them, advised, his concrete jaw and hollow cheeks set firm,

"Good," he replied and then laughed. "Mind you, I'm Nderim Sallaku. I don't think anyone in authority is going to ask me where my car comes from."

He reached out a stubby hand and adjusted the wing mirror down to where he could use it effectively.

"I trust negotiations went smoothly?" he enquired, leaning his head towards them expectantly.

"No problems. It comes from Italy. With the war on the passage was easy."

He got out and clapped his hands together. "I want to take it for a spin, see what it can do."

"I'll come with you," Plator said.

"No. I want my son to see this. Fetch Zamir, tell him his father needs him."

Plator scuttled off while Nderim lit a cigar and strolled across the drive to look out on his estate. It stretched down and swept wide. This was the capital of his kingdom, a little empire in which his activities were well hidden. He yawned. His mouth was big. He'd used to great effect last night in a meeting that stretched through to dawn. By the end of it a great deal of money had changed hands, making Nderim all the richer and some sad end user all the poorer and sicker.

Zamir emerged, paused by the Jensen and shook his head. He was a smaller version of the father without such roundness. A sharper, younger man, dressed more casually although the denim was Levi and the jacket would be beyond the reach of most Albanians.

"What do you think? Nderim asked, gesturing at the car with an open arm.

"Do you need another one, father? You got that new Land Rover only recently."

"Need?" he queried. "I don't need, I want. And I get."

"Some unfortunate soul has lost out."

"What do you mean?"

"It'll be stolen, like all the others."

"I have the papers."

"You have a nephew who controls the officials."

Nderim laughed heartily. "You trying one of your good boy crusades again? Remember what keeps you living like this in a poor country."

158

Zamir folded his arms in frustration.

"Anyway, stop standing there like some religious statue. The birds will shit on you. I'm going for a drive and you're coming along."

"Must I?"

"Better than playing with yourself and watching MTV."

Nderim went to the car and Zamir knew he was expected to follow. His father didn't tolerate disobedience from anyone. Although Zamir was sure he wouldn't end up going missing like some others who displeased his father, he felt it wise to comply.

He sat beside Nderim and watched him fiddle with knobs and flick switches with childlike joy. The wipers set off furiously and he chuckled. When the engine roared to life he became more serious, holding out his hand to ensure they both listened carefully.

"Hear that?"

Zamir was bewildered. "What?"

"Chrysler built. American you know."

"Shall we get going?"

"Yes, you're right, we'll appreciate it better on the move."

Zamir was relieved. He had more studying he wanted to do before hooking up with some friends later. As the gates swung open, he hoped this trip would be short and his father wouldn't think of any jobs he needed doing.

"It's a shame we can't drive one of those big American roads," Nderim said. "We could really fly."

They seemed to be doing quite adequately here, Zamir thought, as they increased speed rapidly, the sharp corners forcing him across the big red seat and straining his seatbelt.

His father was not wearing his. He rocked and rolled, relishing each turn of the wheel as if this was a fairground ride. Down into the valley they went, through crumbling settlements that looked desperately deprived, the damage of the past still clinging to the tired faces that watched them pass.

159

"A new Albania can't come too soon," Zamir commented.

"They chase a rainbow without much hope. Albania will stay in the shadows of Europe where it has long been. We must make our own way."

"What would you have them do?"

Nderim shrugged carelessly. "Like our neighbours, we shouldn't expect any great change of fortune."

"It doesn't affect us."

"Exactly. As long as I can be a business man."

Onwards they sped, Nderim keen to burn fuel and let the car take him away. He was constantly examining the dials or adjusting something to gauge the effect. With his eyes off the road it was a wonder he saw the young girl at all, let alone managed to avoid her. She came out from behind a rusting van parked in a village street and kept on going like she was intent on getting run over.

"Watch out!" Zamir screamed.

His father did not brake but his driving skills were refined enough to make the necessary manoeuvre appear easy.

"That was close!" Zamir said, turning to check behind them to see that she was safe and still chasing her ball.

"No big deal," Nderim sniffed. "If I'd hit her it would have saved her from the shit life is likely to bring."

His coldness was no act. Zamir had seen it so often; a complete lack of sensitivity in acceptance of a harsh reality. The reason likely lay in the past, a fractured upbringing that had prepared him to fight and win in an oppressive country. He spoke very little about his childhood, but his mother, who lived with them, displayed very little affection and spoke only of the hard times she had endured.

And now he had money enough for expensive toys and nothing was going to stop him enjoying them.

"Under that bonnet is the power to tame a storm!" he cried, slapping the steering wheel with glee.

Zamir was pleased when they began the climb homewards. Too long in his old man's clutches made him feel like screaming. He shook inside. If only they'd had this much time together when he was younger, before he was expected to understand their world. Back then his dad was just that big strong guy with the pistol in his bedside table and not the selfish bully he recognised now.

"You can talk to me, you know," Nderim said.

"Sorry, I thought you were too busy congratulating yourself on your new acquisition."

The bigger man stared at his junior, waiting for a genuine apology for that stupid remark. None was forthcoming.

"There's a few things not quite right. I don't think the last owner maintained it much. Air conditioning needs servicing and cruise control isn't working. I'll get Plator to check the fuse box too."

"Do you ever look at yourself in the mirror?" Zamir asked, his blood simmering.

"Yeah, I see a clever guy."

"You complain about whoever had this car last yet you stole it from them."

"I didn't steal anything."

"I've heard Meriton talking about it. You use some for jobs and the best ones you keep."

"So? It pays."

It was Zamir's turn to stare. There were more shadows in his father's tight heart than there were in a graveyard on a sunny afternoon.

"Shouldn't we share some of our wealth with our fellow countrymen?"

"I employ lots of people. That helps the community."

Zamir knew his father was not joking. "I'll be glad to get away to college," he sighed.

"You still think that's the best way forward?"

"Yes. An honest living. Maybe in America or England."

Nderim tutted.

"What?"

"You and your books. The only paper I trust is money."

"There are many ways to earn it."

"That's true, I'll give you that. You're a clever lad, I've always said as much. You should listen to what is on offer though. There's a share in the business for you, if you stay."

"I'm dreaming of other things."

The car was quiet for a minute, apart from the solid grind of the engine as they soared over the final ridge to reveal home lying in front of them. Nderim took a deep breath and his round frame expanded. "I'll see you through all your schooling, pay the fees, because I'm a good father. I'll respect your decision. But don't forget this. In return I expect favours, to honour the family, so don't climb too high onto that self righteous pedestal as the fall can be deadly."

"Yes, father, I understand," Zamir said, very keen to make clear his sincerity.

~

The triumphant return, with spinning wheels sending stones backwards in a shower of power, was short lived. Plator wore a grave expression and Nderim was quick to find out why.

"There's been some trouble," Plator reported, his concern increasing the skeletal appearance of his haunted face.

"Facts," Nderim demanded.

"The law. Clirim's been picked up."

Zamir judged by his father's reaction that this was serious. He had stopped dead in his tracks and rubbed his sizeable neck while the formidable eyebrows creased together.

162

"What was he carrying?"

"The usual."

"Okay, we need a plan." Nderim pointed at the other man standing by the door. "Call Lavdrim. Get him down there, tell him to make sure we aren't linked to this at all."

Now they marched. Zamir kept up with them. This was genuinely interesting. In the hallway their progress was halted by Grandma. She approached slowly but steadily on her stick, her skin wrinkled, browner than theirs with darker patches on her cheeks, neck and arms. Her hair was miraculously still black despite her eighty eight years. The eyes, that fixed on you without blinking, overcame bags and sags by burning brightly. Though there were many small flowers in the pattern of her dress, it did not throw off any cheer. All the colour of this woman's life had been dulled by the years of working the land and her hands and back were buckled as further proof.

"Deri," she said. Only she called him this.

"Yes, mother."

"I don't like the veal you ordered."

He put a hand gently on her shoulder, only to have her push it off again.

"It will spoil the stew."

"I'm sure it's fine."

"I told them to cook the beef instead but they don't listen to me, they are stupid!"

Nderim scowled and ground his teeth. Zamir was amused.

"I'll come to the kitchen soon," he assured her. "I have some business to attend to first."

"Oh, always something else. You forget your old ma!"

"I assure you, I could never do that."

163

He smiled, thinly, at his own irony.   The old woman did not notice any of this. She shook her head, thumped her stick on the wooden floor and searched somewhere in the distance for the answer.

"The stew will be ruined!"

Nderim looked around for the answer and noticed Zamir. "Son, go with your grandma. See if you can set this straight. I'm sure the meat is fine."

"The veal is very poor!" she wailed.

Zamir wasn't keen to take her on when she was in this mood. "Can't I stay with you?" he asked his father. "I'd like to help."

Nderim was heartened by his son's sudden interest. "Okay, we're going into the office."

"I'll come too," grandma decided, gripping Zamir's arm like a vice.

"It's just boring stuff, mother," Nderim said. "You know I don't want you getting involved. You need lots of rest."

She pulled Zamir down to her level. Her beady eyes were screwed tight and latched onto his. "You see, no one cares any more. I'm kept out of everything."

"I'll come and find you as soon as we're finished, I promise," Zamir pledged. "We'll save the dinner, I'm sure."

She was a terrifying edifice of centuries gone, imprisoning the feelings of hope and love because it had become easier than allowing them to run free and risk a flood of the foundations of cast iron strength a nation stood upon.

"Children these days," she hissed. "They have no substance."

She took herself off, mumbling incoherently. Nderim shook his head after her.

"She gets worse," he observed. "Poor mama."

Plator began to wring his long fingers together. Nderim nodded. "To business," he said.

Once securely enclosed behind the varnished wooden panels of the office, Nderim could unleash his power. Zamir stood meekly to one side.

164

"Clirim has been betrayed. He's one of us. We hold together. I will kill the person responsible."

"It could have been a lucky hit," Plator suggested.

"Lucky? How could you ever get that lucky?"

Nderim sat against his expansive desk and picked up a brass paperweight, dropping it continuously from one hand to the other as he spoke.

"If they link him to what happened last month we'll drop him."

Zamir was appalled. "You just called him one of us? Now you say you'll drop him?"

"To protect everyone else, you included," Nderim stated, with a satanic stare.

"What happened last month?" Zamir asked.

Nderim glanced at Plator and then grimaced. "Never you mind. Lavdrim will keep us clean."

Zamir ran a troubled hand through his coarse, curly hair. There was so much secrecy in the business. He longed to distance himself from it.

Nderim began to pace around, his face twitching while he weighed up the threats. "So what have the police done since they picked up Clirim?"

"They came to the cigarette warehouse," Plator advised.

Nderim flushed red with anger. "Did they find anything?"

"Don't think so. We checked out fine. But it's getting hotter."

"We'll have to close that down for a while, start using the shop. We can put Zamir out front. He's purer than white."

Zamir frowned. He wasn't clear what this all meant. They were both looking at him waiting for a response. It suddenly felt very warm in his dad's office.

"I can help, I said as much," he decided.

"Good," Nderim replied, and looked at his watch. "See to it, Plator."

"One thing," Zamir added. They both stopped in their busy tracks. "There's no drugs is there?"

Plator shuffled his long legs. Nderim scratched his belly, came up to Zamir and put a hand on each shoulder.

"Zamir. I hate drugs. I have nothing to do with them, ever. I promise you."

CHAPTER TWENTY THREE

"Zamir, you be polite to everyone tonight, you hear?"

"Of course," he replied.

The boy was stretched out on his bed watching some western pop band jump about to a lively song. Nderim appeared unconvinced because his son's response matched too closely his languid pose.

"I mean it. Top people will be here. They don't need your own brand of virtuous sarcasm."

"It might do them good," Zamir said, without taking his eyes off the screen.

"Maybe. But it won't do us any good."

He looked at his father, who was holding a large whisky in his pudgy hand, and tried to think of another witty retort. Just then his mother came in. Nderim was effusive in his admiration of her appearance.

"Doesn't she look beautiful? I bought the dress for her in Rome."

Nderim treated her like a doll and expected the same approach from all whom they met. To the black hole of his eyes she shone. Others could never quite see it and would laugh at his inane compliments, although not in his sight.

Zamir remaining laid out, lifted his head enough to take her in. No, she wasn't beautiful. Anything but. If you took away the expensive jewellery and the layers of makeup, you'd be left with a very plain looking woman. Mouth too wide, features not evenly set, chin sagging, neck unusually long. Not blessed at all, Zamir always thought.

No bond had ever been established between them. She was inattentive when he was small, leaving various nannies to care for him. As he grew up, Zamir loved her as a mother but found her disappointing. She took no care to learn about the world or gave a single thought to how bizarre it was to be an island of wealth in an ocean robbed of all expectation. He would try to share his thoughts and receive a very blank reaction. She wanted him to be

167

happy without having to make the intellectual effort of understanding. It had been Zamir's first lesson in what to expect from life. Respecting your family was a must regardless of what you thought of them as people.

"Do a spin round, Luriana, see how the hem ripples," Nderim urged.

After she had obliged they looked to Zamir for his approval.

"Very nice," he said, forming a smile.

Luriana laughed, a strangely nasal noise, as she always did when she was the centre of attention. Zamir wished she didn't wallow in the constant exaltation so readily. Surely she knew so much of it was forced?

"I can't wait for the fun to start!" she cried.

"You're going to knock them dead," Nderim assured her. "The hostess with the mostest!"

Zamir rubbed his temples to seek relief. This was just the kind of behaviour that annoyed him. She wriggled her bare shoulders and waited expectantly for the kiss that came.

"They'll all be jealous of me," Nderim said. "The man with the gorgeous wife."

He pinched her bottom and she squealed with delight.

"Good grief," Zamir muttered and went back to the television screen, where a truly attractive young woman in hot pants was waving a shapelier arse at the camera.

~

The party started when the first guests arrived. They, like each that followed, had to pass the Jensen parked virtually across the doorway and illuminated by lamps to ensure it could not be missed. Once inside they were greeted in person by a bullish Nderim and foppish Luriana before being shown through the drawing room to the patio overlooking the garden. It was a splendid August evening with the moon large and bright and just a delicate breeze from the Mediterranean rippling through the warm air.

168

Zamir, whose job it was to ensure everyone was offered something to nibble and drink by the many staff that prowled with trays, found the guests that came through a fascinating mix of serious, stunning, proud and plain ridiculous. Of the more stern looking ones, at least two he recognised as parliament officials, another as an army officer. There was also a leading property magnate, as well as the head of a lorry haulage company.

Most of the younger women were striking but unfortunately a little too aware of the fact to actually qualify in his book as attractive. Older wives tried to compete and these were the most absurd. Maintaining a place at the top of society was always a precarious task.

A girl of note, with great swirls of dark hair floating across the bare back of her stunning white and green dress, was his father's personal assistant, Flutura. She never missed a social occasion and often accompanied Nderim on trips across the border. Zamir knew that she could afford those pretty clothes with the copious salary she received. What she did for her father in return, Zamir preferred to not discover.

As people fanned out around the pool, the water twinkling like silk in the lights, Zamir sat in a lounger and put his hands behind his head. The great dome of the heavens stretched above him and his future felt full of possibilities. His exam results were in and he had excelled himself. The metaphorical ship was soon to sail and his ticket aboard was secure. Law school in wealthy America awaited him, where he could do great good and earn clean money.

He watched the gathered greatness of Albania, so earnest in their intent, and felt no pressure to be a part of it. Those stiff handshakes, meaningful nods, flashes of long legs exposed by short skirts and arms furtively slid around waists, were not his concern. Unfortunately, his reverie was soon disturbed by his father's gravely tones.

"Zamir, to the office, now. There's some business to attend to."

~

169

It was all men who filtered discreetly in to the study. Except, of course, for Flutura. She took her place beside Nderim's chair, her hand on his shoulder while he addressed the room. He was the only one permitted to sit. Zamir leaned against the wood panelling and watched his father control the room. "So tell me your news," he demanded.

The first person to speak was Nderim's brother, Besart. He was a squat figure whose head seemed to have joined his body and done away with a neck. "That tip you gave me for the match won me fourteen thousand lek," he said and chuckled.

Nderim smiled but seemed unimpressed. "I don't wish to speak of chance. I want assurances."

Next up was a government minister, much thinner yet still small. "I've employed some new staff. They'll be easy enough to buy."

Now Nderim was more interested, his copious eyebrows were raised. "You're sure?"

"Pretty much. They can pull the right strings and overlook what we need them to."

"Be sure," Nderim repeated. "Remember that generous amount I put forward to back you is really like a loan. You need to repay me in the right way."

Zamir noticed their neighbour was present. He lent them an underground area carved out of the hillside that was used as storage. In a raid when Zamir was a boy, the police had failed to find this secret place and Nderim had always been grateful. It gave him a strong argument against the press who were adamant of his wrongdoings.

Nderim took a slug of whisky and cleared his throat noisily. "You all saw the car when you came in. That is a demonstration of the reward for success. We all need that kind of blessing. Well, I wanted to assure all of you that business is now going back to normal. I've had quite a burden of worry to carry."

170

Flutura caressed his collar bone while he dropped his head and took a deep breath.

"Clirim was a fool. Lavdrim has been cool. The setback of six months ago, and the scrutiny we got because of it, is in the past. Now we need to make up for lost time. We have a stockpile of tobacco and several cars. They all need to go where they'll be appreciated and paid handsomely for. You all have your part to play."

Zamir was surveying the room and saw many a nod as well some uncomfortable glances. It was clear than no one could refuse, say goodbye to all this clandestine action and walk out. His dad's henchmen guarded the door.

"So we can count on all who are present," his father continued. "That includes you, Zamir."

All heads turned his way suddenly, and they all seemed to be crowned with horns. While he searched for a friendly smile, Nderim got up and joined him. After receiving a resounding pat on the back, Zamir was finding it hard to catch his breath.

"I am most proud of my eldest offspring. He has shone in his studies and will leave us to take them further. Afterwards he intends to secure a top job. Please show your appreciation."

Everyone clapped as a matter of expectation. Zamir had never felt so embarrassed. He was getting the treatment his mother got. The difference was she loved it.

Nderim held up a finger to signal a silence. "But let us temper our congratulations and remember such success is a reflection of the support that family brings. As we give as much as we can to Zamir's future, he returns in effort for us.

"So, I'm pleased to say he will prove just how great a son he is by helping our endeavours. We can count on him to take part in operations on the very front line before he disappears for too many years at college."

171

There was a second round of applause. Meriton, his large uncle, came up to Zamir and hugged him firmly.

"Love a family man," he growled.

Zamir was already in shock and this gesture increased the surreal nature of events. Meriton had spent several years in prison for breaking open someone's skull. In a separate incident, a man had died. Meriton had got off on a technicality but all in the family knew he had murdered him for exposing the business for his own gain. This was someone who attacked people if they irritated him. He terrified Zamir.

Nderim applauded this act of bonding, laughing at the startled look on his son's face, his cigar clenched between the teeth of his grin.

"This has been very warming," he exclaimed. "Now let's get back to the party before we are missed. Eat and drink well, enjoy the hospitality of the hand that feeds you all so willingly."

The room emptied with an almost audible, universal sigh of relief. Flutura went last, out of deference to the domination of the males. She passed close to Zamir, who had been unable to move, reached out and pinched his cheek with her delicately manicured fingers. Expensive perfume flooded his nostrils.

"Who's getting to be a big boy now?" she purred. "I'll keep my eye out for you."

No one noticed that Zamir did not return to the festivities. They even drank to him around midnight without really looking for him. He was buried in his room under the duvet, trying to think of a reason to get out of his obligation. Illness perhaps? He knew this would not wash with his tough guy father. Honesty? Tell him he does not want to be part of anything shady. That would risk his own future. Maybe run away? He snorted at his own stupidity.

He had helped his father in small ways during his teenage, writing up labels, shifting boxes, cleaning cars, fronting the shop. This was all small fry.

172

Never had he travelled or taken the lead on a job. The unethical nature of the business, one that had cradled him through a life of opportunity, now reared its ugly head to test his morality and do battle with his allegiances. Not having to face a choice was still preferable to making one.

He emerged from under his hideout and stared at the ceiling. The mobile of the solar system, which he had made when only eleven, hung over him, still rather clever looking, despite the dust. Those mighty planets each represented a different mood or personality. War, peace, magic, jollity. He knew the classical suite by Holst intimately. Yet the all had the same fate. An eternal circuit around the all dominating sun. They were trapped by gravity and history. He was like one of them, reined in by family. It would take an immense upheaval in the universe to break free.

Later, when the black limousines were filing away through the gates, Zamir managed to find his mother alone in the lounge. She was clearly rather tipsy, unable to sit up straight, stray hair escaping in all directions.

"Where's dad?" he asked.

"He had something to do with Flutura," she said, her head flopping onto a cushion and her eyes closing.

"Doesn't it bother you that he spends so much time with her?"

"Why should it. Your father is very good to me. Besides, I think Plator is with them."

As he sat on the other end of the sofa, Zamir could see Plator out on the drive, discussing something at length with the army officer who was about to get into his car. Zamir decided not to mention it.

"I wanted to ask you something, mother."

"Can't it wait until tomorrow," she replied, a yawn filling the air with the smell of wine.

"No, it's bothering me too much."

He waited for her to show some interest. She began breathing heavier and appeared to be dropping off to sleep.

173

"Mum!"

He tickled her knees. That always got a reaction. She raised her head and pulled a very unflattering expression of irritation.

"What is it?"

Zamir clenched his hands together in earnest. "Dad wants me to help with the business before I go to college."

"So what?"

"I think I'd be better off here, preparing and working through options."

"Does he want you to go away then?"

"Yes. As far as Italy I believe. I'm not sure I'm ready for such an important job."

She looked more confused than ever. "Well, if he thinks you're right for it. He knows best."

"Can you speak to him for me? I'm worried it might be dangerous."

She had shut her eyes again, although the many lines on her face remained quizzical.

"I can't argue. It would hurt him so much if he thought I was disagreeing with his judgment or that you weren't willing to lend a hand."

"It's bound to get complicated and delayed. I might miss an important deadline and lose the place somehow."

"Zamir, leave me alone. Your father loves you. Your father knows best."

CHAPTER TWENTY FOUR

"I don't belong here," Zamir concluded after Plator had finished going through the instructions.

"You will do alright," Plator insisted. "You did the test run yesterday without any mistake."

They were lounging on the beds in their dingy hotel room, Plator smoking heavily and idly flicking through a glossy magazine, Zamir with his hands behind his head but far from relaxed.

"I keep thinking I'm doing wrong."

"Mess up and it will be very wrong."

"Smuggling tobacco is illegal," Zamir stated, as if Plator didn't know.

"It pays. There are plenty of the young and rich in Italy who want it all. We're supplying a market. The government says it's wrong because they lose the tax profit."

Zamir banged a palm down in frustration. "I know I'm going to get caught."

Plator sat up and pointed a yellowing finger at him. "Listen, your father is being very careful about this. That's why we've delayed. He wants to know there is no one on to us. He wouldn't send his own son into the fire."

"I can just imagine myself freezing. I'm so nervous. Didn't you get like that when you started?"

Plator thought about this question for a just a moment. "Maybe. You get used to it in time. I've done your dad's bidding for fifteen years, and before that for others."

Zamir wondered how long his life of crime had stretched. He must be easily sixty, he reckoned, or possibly older judging from the look of him. The shady path had taken its toll. The lies and deceit had drained the colour from his skin and wasted away every last ounce of fat from his flesh.

"Any regrets?" Zamir asked.

175

Now he laughed until the tar on his chest moved up to clog the passage of air. He choked on his own mirth. Eventually, he recovered, wiping his mouth with the cuff of his shirt.

"I'm happy with my lot. The river of blood flows on, I saw the Italians invade, then the German control. Communism brought more suffering, and now Serbs and Croats fight. Keeping to one side of all that has been better. If your father needs something done, I know he has a purpose and I will profit. Nothing more do I need to think about."

"I want to get away completely, find my own fortune abroad."

Plator nodded slowly, a smile forming that linked the caves of his cheekbones. "I think this is good. You are a wise young man. Follow a dream. For me it is too late."

"Really?"

"Oh yes. This is my way now, locked in." He clamped his hands together. "You don't break ranks and stay free."

Zamir thought he caught sight of a tiny flame in his grey eyes. Yet in the dim light of late afternoon, it and him blended with the bland wallpaper until he was nothing more than a dull silhouette of a man.

~

Zamir awoke some time later and the bare yellow bulb was alight on the ceiling. He sat up and felt as if he had left his insides on the bed, so empty did he feel. And he was alone. With a bit of luck, Plator had gone out to fetch some food. He was starving.

The curtains were closed as they had been since they arrived. It was stifling him, being cooped up like this. He wished he could go outside, breathe some fresh air. In here it smelt of body odour and well worn socks.

He went to the sink and splashed some cold water over his face, picked up the book that was the only spark in this enforced cell and let himself fall back onto the bed. He had been reading for over an hour before Plator

176

sidled in. Fortunately, he had brought kebabs. Less uplifting was the news that came with it.

"You go tonight," he said. "Better eat well then get ready." He threw the bag of food onto the pillow by his head.

~

Zamir was buzzing. He had completed the pick up as instructed, the cavernous boot was full. Now Plator had left him to it and he was heading north towards Montenegro. He had been trusted with the Jensen because his father wanted him to have the best and had let him drive it many times especially, to get a feel for the controls. This was the first car in the long line of his dad's acquisitions that Zamir had developed any interest in. It was different, like it infiltrated your personality and made you feel strong. If it wasn't for the cargo he was carrying he would now have been able to revel in power entrusted to him. A dip of his right foot produced heady momentum and a glorious roaring from under the long bonnet. He felt like James Dean and then remembered he had died whilst driving his Porsche. Besides, he had to keep to the back roads to avoid attention in accordance with Plator's instructions, as he was a teenager in a rather expensive motor, so he wasn't able to let the car unwind anyway.

But as he let the speed drop he found himself increasing it again. The imminent danger of getting stopped kept his adrenalin flowing, the sweat making the wheel stick to his hands. Every time he saw another vehicle's lights, whether behind him or coming the other way, his shoulders tightened. The price he would pay for getting caught seemed way too high right now.

"There's a gun in the glove compartment," were Plator's parting words, accompanied by his ghoulish smile.

"Am I licensed to have that with me?" Zamir had screeched to himself after he had driven off.

He shivered when he thought of this again. This was going to be a long trip, all night he reckoned. The rendezvous at Dubrovnik was set for just before dawn. He focused on that moment, the return home and his imminent departure for college. At least he didn't have to go as far as Italy. Something had bothered his father enough to relieve him of that burden. And what could really go wrong in the empty quiet of this night, deep in the unpopulated countryside.

When the rain started, blowing across the wide windscreen in gusts, he shook his head and tried to get the wiper blades working at the right speed. This drizzle could only really help him, he decided, because it kept people inside. For the first time, he felt cold in the big driver's seat.

"You'll look after me won't you baby?" he said to the car, prescribing a female gender like it was now his lover. "Such beauty can only bring good luck."

This statement proved to be incorrect in no time at all. In the beam of the lights Zamir observed the dark frame of a truck turning right out of a junction and moving across his lane. It took the fraction of a second to realise he had not been seen and then slam on the brakes. He was able to stop but the other driver clearly couldn't and in trying to avoid Zamir, careered off the road and down the embankment opposite.

Zamir sat still and stunned. The engine stalled and went dead. By the time he could get out, the world was quiet, as if holding its breath. In the red glow at the back the rain whispered gently. Slowly, he walked round to where the van had tumbled over. In the dark he could see very little, just a large shape.

"Are you okay?" he called

There was no answer.

"Do you need help?"

The eerie emptiness prevailed. What to do next?

"Don't get involved in anything," Plator had drilled into him. "No matter what, stay away. The slightest complication or hitch could lead to ruin."

178

Now Zamir panicked. He had to get moving at once. He got in and after several failed starting attempts, drove off in haste.

"Fuck, fuck, fuck, fuck, fuck," he repeated.

His breathing was intense and heavy. What if there was someone injured down there? They might die because of him. Or be already dead? How would he live with that guilt?

After a few miles he passed a car by the side of the road. In an instant it pulled out behind him. The headlights closed in despite his own extreme speed.

"Piss off," he said to the rear view mirror.

They did no such thing. Instead, whoever it was trailed him meticulously around every bend, dip and rise. This went on for ten minutes, increasing Zamir's anxiety and sending his brain into a whirl of questions. Was there a turning ahead where he might be able to give them the sudden slip? Should he go slow and see if they did?

When the blue flashing light was switched on his decision was made. He would have to lose them. Instinctively, he accelerated. That didn't do the trick. A fork in the road approached. At the last second he chose left. His pursuer was as quick as him.

"Oh, get lost," he shouted.

A steeper hill took him down and he managed to get some distance ahead. When that got big enough for him to be out of sight, he stopped sharply in a lay-by and switched everything off. As if by magic, the other driver fell for his trick and raced past. As soon they had disappeared, he set off again, swinging in a big circle and heading in the opposite direction.

Now he had make sure he didn't end up back at the scene of the accident so he took the first turn right and then right again. When he saw the sign for Koplik he knew he was back on course. A bizarre sense of elation took hold of him. He got the window to buzz down after a few pushes and held his head out into the spray.

179

"Give 'em hell you creature of the night!" he shouted.

His freshly soaring blood froze immediately when he saw the road block ahead. Mortified, his limbs became solid too. The car hurtled on. He saw army personnel with guns at the ready.

This was enough to galvanise his driving impulses. He took back control and turned the wheel sharply. Unluckily, he had left it all too late. There was a shattering crunch as he hit a wooden barrier and the whole venture came to a standstill.

Through the open window a concerned soldier spoke to him in Albanian.

"You okay, son?"

"Yes," Zamir said, strangely calm. "I need a drink of water."

"Can you move?" he asked. "Does anything hurt?"

"My arm. And my foot."

"You need to get out if you can. This thing might blow, there's petrol spilling."

"Right, I will," Zamir said, obediently.

"This door's crushed in, you best try the other."

As Zamir climbed out a police car drove up. An officer got out of each side and walked with great purpose to where Zamir was standing.

"Well, you've given us the run around but we have you now. You're in a lot of trouble."

~

The entire room was featureless, grey and small. Zamir sat nervously in a very uncomfortable little wooden chair, biting his lip and waiting for something to happen. Since being brought here he had seen no one except the one bored looking guy who was stood opposite, staring sightlessly. Zamir worried that he might get beaten and bashed around. The opposite appeared to be the priority. From what he could make of communications on the journey here, he was marked as a priority and great care was to be taken.

180

There was a similar chair opposite him, separated by a square table. This indicated to Zamir that some sort of interrogation was imminent. With a dry mouth and his mind whirling, Zamir tried to think of what questions might be asked and how he should best answer them. He had to suppose he was alone in this mess until he heard otherwise.

One blessing was that the pains he had when he climbed out of the car were fading. What was going to hurt most was losing his freedom and all that he wanted to do. His dark thoughts were disturbed by the door opening.

A bald man with a pointed nose and chin came in, his beady eyes not leaving Zamir for a moment. He threw a brown packet onto to the desk and sat down, leaning immediately forward to maintain his staring with thin arms crossed.

"Congratulations, Zamir," he said. "You're in the deepest shit possible."

Zamir looked away and remained silent.

"What's a boy of your age doing getting mixed up in this? You should be playing soccer and chasing girls."

Zamir went to construct an answer, then stopped himself. He wasn't used to being quiet.

"You know what's in the package?"

Zamir glanced at it and shrugged.

"I'll show you."

From within he pulled out a bag of off white powder, wrapped with lots of cellophane. Zamir was horrified enough for it to show.

"Well, as you seem surprised, I'll tell you. That is heroin."

Zamir reached out and picked the packet up, as if he needed the touch it to satisfy himself there was no illusion.

"That amount you've got there is enough to destroy a life. Whether through using the drug or doing something bad to get the money to pay for the pleasure."

Zamir threw the package back down onto the desk in revulsion.

"In the back of your car was over a hundred times more. One hundred! One hundred lives ruined, at least. One hundred victims and everyone around them affected."

The police officer's voice had climbed high and strong as he spoke, the accusatory tone designed to pierce Zamir through the heart.

"So you think it's alright, smuggling crap like this?" he demanded, leaning across to bring their faces close together.

Zamir could smell mint on the man's breath. He reminded him of a favourite teacher from school who was quite strict. It was always one of the other pupils getting corrected. This morning it was him.

"No, I don't," Zamir admitted, his throat crackling with tension.

"So why were you doing it?"

"I thought...."

"Yes?"

"I thought it was something else."

"Such as?"

Zamir tried to lean away. His accuser's head followed his movement and kept their foreheads in line.

"Tobacco," Zamir mumbled.

"Oh! Cigarettes. So that is okay. The laws about tax don't matter."

"They do."

"You're not much of a crook. Or are you saying you're innocent?"

"No."

"You have a conscience?"

"I do."

"I don't understand how you can have?"

Now the police officer stood up and began to pace the small space available, his hands clenched together with the knuckles pressed to his chin. Zamir watched him go back and forth, waiting for the next verbal onslaught.

"For such a caring citizen the list of crimes is staggering. Carrying illegal drugs with the intention of crossing the border. In possession of a firearm without a licence. Ignoring an army roadblock and damaging their equipment. Speeding on the highway. Ignoring a police car requesting that you stop. Leaving the scene of an accident without reporting it. Driving a car without insurance."

Zamir closed his eyes, in hope that his tears might not emerge. A child unable to escape his bad deeds.

"In other words, you're fucked," he heard the man say.

All the tension of the last few hours overtook Zamir now, swamping his young body with filthy shame. He shook and clung on to himself hard, terrified that if he let go he might spill out all over the bland floor. When he finally looked up from his huddled disarray, he saw actual compassion.

"Would you like a drink? Coffee perhaps?"

Zamir rocked in the chair enough to indicate that he would. His gradual unravelling from within continued until the cup was put in front of him. The aroma itself was reviving. When he drank, the hot liquid burned his lips and throat.

"I can offer you a way out."

Zamir wanted to cry. It was cruel to be teased like this.

"No really, I mean it."

Zamir bit his lip. "How?" he said, weakly.

"Well, you see, you can get away with anything unless you get caught. That I've done with you, except you're not the one I'm after. It is obvious you've been strung up for this, duped, led in and let down. The real perpetrator is untouched.

"But notice, I've not charged you with a single crime as yet. We don't need to do that. Then we won't get lawyers involved and we can talk man to man."

"What do you want?" Zamir asked.

183

"Not the monkey. You tell me all about the organ grinder. The man that battered Jensen in my compound outside 'belongs' to. Your father? Give me what you know and I'll see that you go free, get on with a true life, and be who you want to be."

Zamir understood the magnitude of this request at once. This would be an act of betrayal to his family. He had a vision of his father leaving court in handcuffs, snarling at him and promising retribution. His mother he imagined whining that her allowance had been cut off. Grandma, confused and angry, might hit him with a walking stick. So much hate sent his way.

"I'd be dead within weeks," Zamir concluded.

"Not if I have my way," the police man insisted, with clear confidence.

Zamir sighed and shook his head slowly.

"Think of all the people you'd be saving from a miserable future. This is your chance to do some real good, go from blame and culpability to being heralded as strong, a credit to yourself."

Zamir clenched his hands together and planted them firmly on the table, his features stony and intense.

"I agree. I'm ready."

CHAPTER TWENTY FIVE

Carol would have loved to have seen the Jensen again, taken one last ride in those big deep seats, feel the leather on the back of her legs as they vibrated in tune with the rumble of the engine. With the sick irony that only death can wield, the car was returned only days after Richie had watched the life drain from her, breath by strangled breath.

"I want it looked after properly," she had told him when the news came from abroad, her glassy eyes turning on him beside the bed.

"Is that a dig at me?"

She waved a tired, thin hand in his direction. "You know what I mean."

"I'm not sure I do. I lost it after all."

"Don't keep carrying that guilt around. Would you have come back home when you did if that hadn't happened? You'd have hated yourself for not being here for me once I got this ill."

Her logic diminished his irritation. He sat down and patted her on the shoulder, feeling the bones through her nightdress.

"As usual, my motives are a mess. I keep on reacting to events and never have any control."

"Once I've gone you can start again, find a fresh path."

"Don't talk like that."

"You know it won't be long now. Cancer doesn't let you go free once you've lost the battle."

Richie was unable to form a response. He knew she spoke the truth with more bravery than he was finding. His sinking heart fell to the floor, where he kicked it around with his agitated feet. Unbeknown to him, she was watching his terror and even now, in her fading hours, sought to help him. She understood his contradictions so much better than he did.

"I'm hoping dad will come and see you again soon," he said.

Her mouth straightened into a hard line. "Once was enough," she stated.

185

"But–"

"He hasn't got a bone of emotion in his body. He intimated that I'd got like this because of my hedonistic lifestyle! I'd hoped for something warm, a touch on my arm, a kiss like the ones he gave me when he really wanted me. Or he might have alluded to my beauty when we got married. Instead it was all practical. Was I comfortable, did I want to move to a private hospital?

"That has always been his problem. It's one thing being so matter–of–fact, to keep being like it when a few lies would be helpful, I can't forgive him for that."

Richie wanted to offer a kind thought to defend his father, to make his mum feel better about it all. He couldn't think of anything good he could justify. As usual, the truth was betrayed by the unsaid.

"If they get the car back in time, will you take me for a drive?"

"Of course," he agreed instantly, boosted by the thought of a purpose. "Where to?"

"Somewhere calm, with a big view where all the buildings and cows look like little models, where I can see the whole world going about its business."

"Yes, we'll do that."

He wanted to sound convincing, as much for himself as for her. She was so pale and ghostly and frail it was difficult to imagine her ever getting up again. Her skin no longer fitted her frame, appearing either stretched or baggy. Maybe the Jensen would revive her one more time.

Fortunately, her mind had stayed sharp and when she was awake she would lie watching the clouds through the window until a thought struck her and they would chat about it for ages. He still clung to her every word. These were the moments that stayed with him the most, what he held onto once she had gone. Not the earrings, a plush rug from Germany, her collection of shells or the wizard coffee machine. These musings and ramblings with

186

their hands entwined, when neither had any other place they could be but together, became special.

"You know how much I sleep now," she said, one bright afternoon near the end. "Well, I dream more than ever. And, of course, you can do anything then. I walk out of here. That's the best thing. Running with strong legs until I go so fast I start to fly. Or I dive off somewhere high, into deep water, and swim like I never could, with the fish and dolphins. It's funny how the mind works, not accepting the limitations of reality."

"Nice thoughts," Richie said, while he was trying to get her to take another mouthful of her dinner.

"More than that. It's essential. Like being in the Jensen once more. Dreams keep you going."

"I don't have any."

"Then make some. And soon or you'll be lost forever."

She pushed the plate of food away and he sank forward with despair.

~

So when the car was returned, Richie watched it unloaded from the big truck with twitchy tension. The paintwork glittered in the bright sunlight like an exotic hummingbird. It demanded a great welcome, as a survivor of a great escapade. The kind of reception Carol would have given. The kind Richie could not manage. He was too far down in a pit of grief, short of sleep and nothing to see ahead except cracks in the foundation of his existence.

As it was he took a cursory stroll from bumper to boot, noted the large dent in the door and the temporary cover over the shattered window, signed the paperwork before turning his back and heading back inside.

And there it sat, dominating the driveway of Carol's house while Richie festered within, shunning a world that had claimed his mother for no discernible reason. Memories returned spasmodically as he picked through her photographs he had scattered across the floor. He found her biggest smiles in the ones taken with the Jensen and realised that although having a son was important to her, her true golden age was the time spent at the wheel of her beloved motor. That was when she was Carol the person, not the mother, or wife, daughter or friend.

In the flicker of the television screen he ate fitfully and let the hours drift past. He was unable to watch anything with any emotional content, switching channels with a rare rush of energy. His mouth was dry, from the strange mix of sweet love and bitter loss. When night fell, too often, he curled up on the sofa listening to the howl of cats and the long spells of silence, chewing his sore fingers.

One morning, there was a knock at the door; he ignored it. When it persisted, he swore until he finally gave in, snatching at the handle and revealing a bulky older man with large, intense eyes and arms covered with tattoos. Richie thought he was vaguely familiar.

"Yes?" he demanded.

"I....err....hope I'm not intruding."

"You are," Richie said, simply.

"Sorry," the man mumbled and shuffled backwards. "I should have taken the closed curtains as a sign. Only I've been gathering the courage to call for so long."

"What did you want?"

Richie was irritated and sensed this might be an opportunity to unleash some of his anger. The big guy's brow furrowed and his lips tightened.

"I was a friend of your mother's," he said. "From a while ago."

"School?" Richie conjectured.

He growled a laugh. "No. Not that far back. I met her just after she got that car."

"You're Joe!"

"You know my name?"

For the first time in months Richie felt a smile form. "She kept your business card on her notice board. It's still there now, Joe's Parlour with the snake motif."

Joe's eyes widened even further. "I never thought....did she ever say much about me?"

"Sometimes, I think she had some guilt about leaving you behind."

Joe broke down at this point, reaching out with a colourful arm to steady himself on the door frame. Richie patted him on the shoulder, unsure of how to deal with the situation. To his relief, Joe seemed determined to maintain his dignity.

"I'm sorry. You just buried your mother and I'm here weeping like a baby."

"So you know she passed away."

"Yes." Joe bit his lip to stifle in an effort to hold himself together. "I knew her for just twenty four hours," he continued.

"Well, you made a big impression in only one day."

Joe clearly liked this assessment for he recovered his spirits a little, standing up and straightening his beard.

"It damn nearly made me go under," he told Richie. "I'd lost in love when I was younger, I thought Carol was my saviour. She had other plans. I'm relieved to hear I was a positive influence on her."

"You were the catalyst for much more. It must have been a momentous night."

"It was." Joe glanced away for a moment. "How much did she tell you?"

"Enough. She got a tattoo. Everyone was amazed by that, like we never knew her."

Joe eyes glowed with the memory. "I guess I saw bits of her you never did."

Richie shuddered. "More than I need to hear."

"Oh but it was beautiful....she was beautiful."

The two of them fitted this thought in with their deeply personal image of the woman, creating a silence that endured as each wondered what to say next.

"I was at the funeral," Joe said, eventually.

"Really? That must be where I recognise you from. You should have made yourself known to me."

"No. Not there. Not my place. I stayed at the back. Your dad was there."

"Him," Richie sniffed. "In body, not mind. I'd had rather chatted to you."

"From the little bit you spoke of it sounds like she had an unbelievable adventure in that car."

"Oh, she did. Lived life to the full. Until it was taken away. I think she guessed her fate when she came back to England."

"Really?"

"Completely."

They shared this notion in quiet agreement. Joe shuffled uncomfortably.

"I'd love to hear more. Maybe I can pop back another day?"

"Come in now," Richie declared.

"Really?"

Joe coughed nervously as he entered the hallway. When Richie opened the curtains in the lounge, it was as if he'd just broken into the tomb of Tutankhamun, such was Joe's barely concealed rapture. He appeared in awe of the surroundings, stopping to look at every picture or ornament.

"I haven't been keeping the place very tidy. It's so hard," Richie said as he watched this bear of a man attend to every detail with delicate interest.

"Don't worry, I'm not an organised person and you've had such grief to deal with."

"Haven't we all," Richie sighed, touching one of Carol's photographs with his toe.

"Yes," Joe agreed, with a stiff nod.

Carol was there again with them, pulling at their fragile heart strings.

"Coffee?" Richie suggested. "My mum has....had....the most amazing machine."

"Yes please," Joe replied, his sadness allayed by the welcome.

190

"Can't offer you much else, I've used up her supplies."

The two of them sat through a couple of drinks and hours while the son gave an account of Carol's life to the lover, especially the years spent in Europe. Richie amazed himself how easily he found it to speak of her and once he realised how therapeutic it was, he was keen to highlight every aspect. Joe was attentive throughout, not at all phased or distressed by references to her romantic attachments. To the contrary, he expressed delight to hear of her carefree existence and many suitors.

By the time he got to the point when she returned home, Richie felt much admiration for Joe and was reassured once again by his mother's taste in friends, later in life. Richie shook his hand warmly when he stood up to leave, Joe's slim fingers returning the firmness of the gesture. It was a shame he had to go.

Once outside, they lingered by the car making small talk. Joe plunged his hands into his pockets and gazed off up the road.

"Well, it's been a pleasure to meet Carol's son and get a glimpse inside her place."

"No, the pleasure's been mine. I think I needed to talk to someone about the good stuff."

Joe took a deep breath. "So, here it is, the thing that set all this in motion." They both turned to face the car. Richie saw his final days in Siena and how the devil within him had destroyed his relationship with Alessia. He recalled their drive into the mountains, pulling her little white dress off over her head and tumbling to the ground together. Then her final words came back to him. "I mean it. Don't call here again."

"Stupid thing," he said to Joe. "Caused me nothing but trouble."

Joe in the meantime was also reminded of great passion. Carol had been so excited by their trip to that remote spot, completed by her legs up surrender to him. She would be forever fresh in his mind in that exquisite moment.

191

"It's fabulous," Joe said.

"Really?" Richie questioned. "Didn't your heart break when you saw her drive away?"

"I never watched her go, only come."

"Oh."

Richie tried to imagine the final scene between them. He had always admired his mother's ability to blaze her own trail. Looking at poor Joe now, he had to conclude that she had been a bit of a bitch to leave him in such a mess.

"Is it in working order? That's quite a dent."

Richie followed Joe to the damaged door. "I don't know."

Joe considered him for a moment. "Sorry. I guess you've had other stuff on your mind."

"My own wreckage."

Joe smiled briefly at his analogy. "Could I sit in it one last time?"

Richie went back inside and returned with the keys. When he was unable to get in from the driver's side they went round to the passenger door. Joe sank into the seat with a satisfied moan.

"Oh yes," he growled, running his hand across the dashboard.

Richie, leaning down, sighed. "I don't know. It's sat here for the last fortnight and I've not once felt the urge to come out here for even a look."

"What will you do in the long run? Keep it as a monument to her?"

"I've no fucking clue. One of her dying wishes was that it be well looked after. I had thought someone might be able to use it for parts but I'll have to pay for the repair, she'd already claimed the loss with the insurance company. Then I'll sell it, I suppose, to someone who's keen. They're worth quite a bit."

"No! You must not!" Richie took a step away from his ardent reaction.

"Keep it for yourself," Joe continued.

"No thanks. I'd rather give it to you."

A shocked expression passed over Joe's face. Richie, observing him from a few feet away, concluded that he looked quite the part, stretched out across the red leather.

"That would be too generous," Joe said.

"Not at all," Richie countered. "You'd be very welcome. Take it away as you see it, sort out the repair and I'd be happy."

The astonishment still dominated Joe's countenance as he quickly pulled himself out as if he was trespassing by having contact with the car.

"I'm serious. Mum would be delighted. Her beloved Jensen being cherished by her beloved Joe."

Joe shook his head but the situation remained unchanged. He had come here seeking some small connection with the past and was now being offered something much more lasting.

"Do you know what happened after it was stolen, I mean, I can see there was an accident. A joy ride?" he wondered.

"No, nothing that simple. I'm rather afraid it might put you off."

"I'd like to know the facts."

Richie felt he had to tell him. "Okay. It ended up being used by a crook linked with the Mafia. A man was arrested when he crashed it trying to take drugs out of Albania. There was quite a big court case. The guy got to leave the country in return for all the details of his father's operations and those involved.

"It was all rather sordid. I don't think the story helped me warm to the car again. Mum knew it was coming back and wanted me to take her for a drive to a spot with a big sky and a long view. She didn't live long enough."

"If only," Joe mused, glancing across the glimmering paintwork. "All right. You haven't said anything that would stop me taking you up on your fantastic gesture."

Richie extended a hand, which Joe grabbed at vigorously, drawing them into a hug they both seemed to need. When they pulled apart, neither of them could hold back a grin that poured from the heart.

CHAPTER TWENTY SIX

"You couldn't invent this," Joe laughed as he drove the great Jensen out into the hills. "I hope you're comfortable my darling Carol."

He glanced at the seat beside him where a long box lay, inside which Carol's remains shifted and settled with each corner. They headed to a place Joe knew well. The road flattened out and ran along a long grassy ridge. Below, the ground swept away in vast swathes of grass covered with the cheerful yellow of buttercups.

From the car park he carried her to a bench just beyond the stile. From here they could look out on church spires, stands of tall trees, a patchwork quilt of fields and a river snaking with a gleam in the afternoon sun. A multitude of lives were playing out across this vast canvas, too small to be seen but no less important for that. Kids would be skipping home from school or finding reasons not to, adults hiding out while others babbled gossip into telephones. Just as someone reached a moment when plans fell into place, a near neighbour might have gone blind. Contradictions and agreements at every turn. They were all carrying on, oblivious to Carol and her life of adventure.

A woman with a dog approached and seemed to slow down, ready to chat. Joe had a friendly air in old age. His wiry curls were very grey now, and grew out a little longer. With the beard he'd let grow, he was like an elderly grizzly bear. His eyes were still big and kind, topped by quizzical brows that had curiously retained their colour. However, when she saw his odd companion she elected to ignore him. Her pet was curious, only to be pulled away and scolded.

Joe did not care. He wasn't here to engage with anyone else. His part today was to let in nature's never ending story, be at one with his surroundings just as Carol would have been.

He let his head hang back. The insects buzzed with electric excitement and a lark hovered up high, frenetic in song. The sky was a magic blue between huge piles of cotton wool clouds that seemed to be close and far away at the same time. A timeless cycle played out without the need to search for a meaning.

"How about this?" he said to the box. "This is what you had in mind I think." The golden rays grew much longer before he returned to the car. It was a sigh of complete satisfaction he released as he turned the wheel back towards Carol's house.

"Better return you to Richie as promised," he said.

He flicked on the radio and a lush, romantic tune rolled out of the speakers, quite out of tune with the Jensen's image of a racy motor. Somewhere along the way, when Joe went to change gear, Carol's hand came to rest on his. When he looked across, she was right there, smiling and stretching out with bliss, just like she had before he kissed her all those years ago.

"You're really here?" he asked her.

"Of course."

"I'm not going mad?"

"No."

"No, I suppose I couldn't be. There's nothing crazy about getting what you want."

"Which is?"

"You next to me."

"I always will be," she replied, reaching out to caress the hair at the back of his neck. "The roar of the engine makes me feel so alive."

~

"Thank you, it's been a special afternoon," Joe said, handing Carol's ashes to Richie on the doorstep. "There was a lot of view and a whole lot more sky. I think she'd have liked the setting."

"Just as she wanted," he was glad to say.

196

"And me," Joe added.

"Well exactly. I could have done it myself, but with much less enthusiasm. My memories of driving that thing are tarnished."

"A shame."

Joe sensed a feeling of unease in Richie. "I'll be off then."

"Won't you stay awhile?" Richie asked.

"No, no."

"We could talk a bit more about her."

Joe chewed his tongue while he contemplated the offer. Richie was clearly still very low. His thin body hung like an empty raincoat on a peg. Joe was keen to maintain the magic of his afternoon with Carol.

"Okay," he concluded. "You can share some more memories."

Once inside the conversation flowed smoothly. They were united by the common purpose of celebrating Carol's life.

"This was my first outing since the repair was done. It seemed fitting."

"So how easy was it to get fixed?"

"Sourcing the parts was the hardest thing, I think. I gave it to a guy in town who I trusted. I'd done all his tattoos so I think he went the extra mile, so to speak, to make things right. It's as good as new on the outside. The interior is wearing a bit but I wanted to leave that it feels personal....intimate. I even left the dent in the dashboard. There's a story to little things like that."

Richie was visibly impressed. "I made the right decision."

"Look, it will always be yours really. The paperwork makes no difference. If you ever fancy a spin or even want it back for good, I'll oblige without argument."

"That would be so weird," Richie said. "I'm never going to want to go near the thing. Come over and see me whenever, no problem, but I won't be rushing out to that car."

"It's the closest I can get to her. I sense her."

197

Joe was careful not to mention how she'd been there with him when they'd hit the open road. It might be too upsetting or disrespectful.

"She's part of the fabric of the thing, like her soul is in the engine," he continued.

"That's her voicing approval. I know, deep down, she didn't want me to be the one to keep it, after the way I lost it so easily."

"I better take great care of it then," Joe said.

"I can see you will."

"I've decided to retire, sell off the salon. So I'll have plenty of time on my usually busy fingers."

"Wow. Perfect."

Richie was genuinely pleased and Joe caught a flash of Carol in the sudden radiance of his smile.

"You won't miss the work then?" Richie wondered.

"Oh, I've been doing it for so long. It'll be strange but I've done my share." He held up his hands and examined the back of them as if he was assessing their career. "To be honest, I think my eyes are going a bit."

"I guess you have to be accurate."

"Did you like your mum's?"

"I'm not much of a one for tattoos. She was proud of it, that's what matters."

"I'll show you one of mine."

Joe sat forward and began to unbutton his shirt, making Richie very obviously uneasy. When Carol's name was revealed above Joe's heart, his concern faded to sadness.

"She really had an impact on you, didn't she?"

"Like a lightning strike. I was never the same."

"I'm sorry she upset you so much."

Joe raised his big eyebrows. "I wouldn't have missed it for the world. You could have a thousand days with someone who was okay and it could never

198

match one with her. And in some weird way, because I lived without her for so long, it doesn't feel so different now. I lost her long ago."

They both glanced at the box of her remains, standing neatly on her expansive German rug.

"What is your plan for her ashes?"

"I'm going back out to Siena, sprinkle them into the dusty Tuscan soil. She never gave me any instructions I just know she was at her happiest there, so that feels right."

Joe suffered a twinge of jealousy that tightened his stomach. Richie was most certainly correct about her special time, he was closest to her after all, it just hurt to hear. Now he needed to leave.

"I wish you good luck with that," he said, standing up and stretching. "I'm going to head off."

When Joe paused in the hallway for another handshake, he saw that the emptiness in Richie's eyes was more than mourning. He was facing a tough stretch ahead, trying to rebuild his life without her. Joe recognised as well as anyone how loss could throw a dark cloud over you, making the signs and answers hard to read.

"It will get easier," Joe assured him. "You're young still and new chances are sure to present themselves."

"Chances to make more mistakes," Richie concluded with a gloomy tone.

"And to change the pattern of the past. Your mother is proof of that."

Joe backed his pride and joy carefully down the drive, content now to devote his remaining years to his shrine on wheels, his road of remembrance clear and straight. Richie was left behind to seek a path he might be able to settle on, the sorrow constantly in attendance, nagging at him, making him stop and relive her dying days, challenging him at every turn along the way.

CHAPTER TWENTY SEVEN

Joe moved to a bungalow on the south coast, built his own shelter for the Jensen at the end of the garden and settled in to a life of ease. When the weather was right, not wet or so dry to throw up dust, he would let the car roll down the stony track he had laid out and emerge at the front gate, onto a road that had to be free from salt and mud, ready for another rural drive. Sometimes it felt as if he was being steered by a determined unseen force. He would arrive at a place he had no knowledge of and invariably have a lovely time. The towns and villages all around, as well as the countryside between them, unravelled before him. He believed he was being guided by Carol. They were exploring together. A new concept for Joe who had hardly ever travelled beyond his place of birth.

The woman he had been with just once was a regular companion. When he was completely relaxed, often on the way back home, he would have long conversations with her about what they had seen.

"I love you the same as I did those many moons ago," he regularly told her. This was perfect and simple for Joe, for he had none of the worries a real relationship brings. His dream partner was never going to go off with someone else, or criticise what he did. They avoided the clichéd and wearied ways of couples who tire of routine, existing as they did in an unchanging cloud of affection.

Joe lived for these outings. The rest of the time was spent on domestic chores, a spot of gardening and reading his favourite books on mythology. On initial meeting, his many tattoos and bulky presence were off putting to most in the community.

However, the sight of him out working on the car in his faded boiler suit and floppy cream hat became a steady object of reassurance to his neighbours. There always seemed to be some little thing that needed tweaking and he kept the bodywork highly polished. Anyone who found time to speak to him encountered a very chatty man, displaying some disbelief to be this lucky and happy with his lot.

"We kind of fuddle along, don't we?" he said to Mrs Edwards, the well manicured lady opposite with a purple rinse colouring her neat hair.

"Do we? What do you mean by fuddle? We aren't drunkards?"

"Well, you know, being old is much the same. We keeping going, in confusion."

He laughed at himself. She pursed his lips instead of smiling. He wiped his brow with a crumpled handkerchief and squinted up at the sun.

"Another warm one," he observed. "Makes your heart feel so glad."

"You seem very content," she remarked.

"I worked for these days," he said. "I might be a bit unadventurous but I like where I am. Others might be off touring the globe. I've no need for that. All I want is here."

And almost without him noticing, the seventeen years since his night with Carol became twenty seven, and then thirty seven. He maintained the same lifestyle, except he began to move a lot slower and struggled to straighten up after a spell under the bonnet.

Eventually the trips in the Jensen became more infrequent. He found he could start the day with the intention of going out and then become too tired. On some prime afternoons he would awaken in a heap on the sofa, the television talking to no one, and realise he'd missed an opportunity. Without the lure of communing with Carol again he might have stopped driving altogether.

~

That autumn was a splendid one. The trees gained their golden shroud very gradually, day by tranquil day. The leaves shouldered the burden of the approaching winter with majesty, glowing strongly with the fire of the sun, a final surge of vigour before death. The first few had surrendered their grip and floated to ground when Joe stood at the front door, his bulk filling the

201

frame despite the bend in his posture. He saw the strength of the light and the canopy of blue sky and felt the Jensen call to him.

He got himself ready, put on the floppy cream hat and made his way to the back of the garden, clutching his flask, only to realise he had forgotten his sandwiches. Once he had retrieved them he approached the car again, only to meet more frustration. The keys remained on their hook in the kitchen.

"Bollocks!" he snarled.

His breathing was laboured on the third attempt. Trying to walk faster made him more unsteady. Mrs Edwards, who missed very little, came out to check he was okay.

"I'm fine," he called back, only to start coughing. He rested his hands on his knees while he recovered, clearing his throat.

"Are you sure?" she persisted, fidgeting with the big necklace she wore as she stood at his fence.

Joe righted himself and rubbed his back. "Yes, yes."

"Where are you off to?"

"A picnic."

"You be careful!"

"It's a picnic not mountain climb!"

He donned his floppy hat to her in respect and disappeared inside the Jensen. She could be intrusive but she cared about him and had a point. The last time he drove was months ago.

His departure was not smooth. He stalled, used too many revs and missed his gear as he pulled away. His audience shook her head while he smiled sarcastically.

"Come on, Joe," he said to himself. "You can still do this."

He felt the energy flowing from the engine, as hungry as ever. Before long, he was on a main road and flying. It was looking after him and Carol knew the way to go. That large, open park, with the huge oak trees. Yes, just the place for a day like this; stretched out on the grass and watching the martins feeding up ready for migration.

At the first major junction, he stopped, checked both ways and then froze. Which way was it? Right, he was certain. Or was it to the left? He waited for the car to decide. He gazed along the dashboard, saw that ever present indent on the passenger side, then made his move.

There was a loud tooting noise and he hit the brake. Looking out of his window he saw a very angry driver who had skidded to a halt barely yards away from impact. With a gasp, he fumbled for first gear and swung around the poor man and quickly away. His heart was throbbing. He was a liability if he did not concentrate properly.

As his pulse settled he felt glad to have chosen correctly back there. He'd be at his destination soon. Except that everything looked unfamiliar. The large business park was new to him, and that supermarket. There was lots of crass advertising on vast hoardings, bus stops and railings, and too many traffic lights.

He'd passed much of this when a siren started up and blue lights flashed in his rear view mirror. This was a noisy town, not at all where he wanted to be. It took him a while to realise the police vehicle behind wanted him to stop. He was quite flustered by the time he had pulled over, gripping the wheel and taking deep breaths.

A knock on his window startled him even further and when he tried to lower the glass the damned thing kept sticking.

"Sorry, I thought I'd fixed that," he said to the fresh faced youth in uniform.

"Are you okay, sir?" the pale skinned lad enquired with a hint of doubt.

"Yes, yes. Just a little lost."

"Are you aware that you went through a red light back there?"

"Err....no, where?"

"At the pedestrian crossing. Fortunately the person who stopped the traffic had already made the other side."

Joe was mortified, his eyes wide. "I'm sorry, officer."

"You need to be more careful,"

"I do," Joe agreed, looking out across the bonnet, imagining what might have happened.

"So where are you heading?"

He tried to recover his wits. The policeman watched him with concern while he searched for the answer. It came into his head like a revelation.

"A big park, very nice, lots of space there."

"There's nowhere in this town like that."

"Back the other way?" Joe wondered.

"Well, yes. If you joined this road from the Downs—"

"Yes, I did!" Joe exclaimed.

"Well, you should have gone left there."

"Thank you. I'll turn round."

The frown returned. "You'd be better to drive on a bit, there's a roundabout you can use."

"Good idea, thank you."

Only now did the face of the law smile on him. "I wish you well," he said, stepping back from the car and saluting him with a touch of a finger to his cap.

Joe was pleased to get away. He negotiated the route as directed and was immensely relieved when the landscape opened out into the broad setting he was seeking. The car purred to a standstill in front of a knee high fence and the sanctuary of nature drew close. The murmur of the breeze in the trees welcomed him, taking him over as he lay out his blanket across the soft grass.

"At least I can't do anyone any harm here," he said to himself, and let out a wheezy chuckle as he lay down.

His coffee from the flask was still hot enough to enjoy and he congratulated his own food.

204

"One thing I can still do is an egg mayonnaise sandwich."

The park was rightly busy on such a fine day. Energetic and sweaty boys were demonstrating their soccer skills while groups of girls, displaying as much flesh as was decent, soaked up the sun and stared at their phones.

"Enjoy, you think you're gonna be young forever," Joe commented. "I'm not sure I'd want to be that age again, with all those lonely years still ahead of me."

He noticed an adolescent couple on a bench nearby. The lad seemed to be very keen on physical contact while his companion was much less comfortable, pulling her skirt tight across her legs. After several transgressions she grew tired of his insistence and walked off, making her suitor follow, full of assurances about of the purity of his desire. Joe laughed, although for them it certainly wasn't funny.

There were lots of small children clearly overjoyed at the chance to run free. With kites, trucks, dolls in little pushchairs and great curiosity they explored, chasing butterflies or running from bees.

"How strange it is being so ancient," Joe remarked. "All I can do is sit and watch. I think I've lost all relevance to the world."

An old woman was wheeled by in a wheelchair, her eyes, set deep and dark, were forlorn, bereft of life until they stirred into strong envy when another elderly lady buzzed by on a mobility scooter. How priorities change with the passing of the decades.

His was a relaxed acceptance of his age. He'd been blessed with so many years of good health and, apart from his sad lack of romantic success, no other trauma had ever touched him. His easy melancholy numbed any possible regrets. He closed his eyes and drifted through happier memories. The shadow of the trees stretched long and the air became chilly. The far horizon he had come here to see grew dark with gathering clouds. They had appeared very quickly.

"Time to leave," he decided.

On the long stretch of road that led across the hills, Carol was beside him.

She patted the dashboard, touching the dials with delicate fingers.

"You've looked after the car so well," she said.

"I did it for you."

"Oh, I think you got a lot from all that tinkering and cleaning."

He glanced at her to catch the electric twinkle in her eyes. He'd always loved the way they shone in the setting sun. She was wearing the same tight jeans he had eased down to do her tattoo. And underneath, he was sure, those pink lace panties he had admired. Her figure was slim. She had stayed the same age as the day she left him.

"You know me so well," he admitted.

"I do. I saw how you struggled today."

"I got confused."

"So maybe it is time to leave the Jensen to rest for good now."

"But....I can't!"

Joe was upset and the car swung dangerously off course and across the road. The gentle squeeze of her palm across his tightened knuckles brought him back on course.

"Don't be scared," she urged. "You've had twenty years. You're tired now."

He swallowed hard and composed himself. "One last run towards home, then."

"Well done, Joe. You're the best man I ever knew."

~

Switching off the engine, Joe sank deep into an eerie silence, sensing an invisible mist had descended. He ran his hands around the firm steering wheel, then dropped them to the seat where he could feel the soft leather in each palm. Taking in a long breath, the scent of wood and burning oil took him back to that night with Carol. He'd been preserving her perfect image throughout the years of waiting, and never did his phone ring to her call.

206

"Carol," he called. "Carol," again his voice chimed out, echoing around the metal frame of the car.

He let his head fall back against the headrest. He understood now she would never answer. It was okay for him to bleed now, the red blood of love to pour from where his heart had been torn in two, just below where her name was burned into the skin. His part in her story had reached a conclusion.

Rain fell hard on the stones of the drive from a sky grown black. Joe was stirred by the noise and opened his eyes again. His neck was stiff in the cold air and though he knew he had legs, he could not feel them.

"Been here a while," he said.

He looked out on a blurry scene, his square little bungalow barely visible. He should go in and make some dinner.

"I guess it doesn't matter."

So he sat out the storm, just inhaling and exhaling calmly until the fall of water reduced to a gentle drip from the edge of the roof of the shelter.

"Right," he concluded.

He gave the gear stick a pat before very deliberately pulling on the catch and hauling himself out on to damp ground. He closed the door carefully and wandered around the car as was his habit, checking all was well.

"Oh, good grief," he grumbled, seeing a splash of mud across the flank.

The marks of a few kamikaze insects on the windscreen produced a similar reaction.

"I can see I need to spend a bit of time up here giving you a good clean. But you deserve it."

He ran his hands along the sleek lines, and marvelled at the abundant power of the shape. This was a car that demanded care and received it like royalty.

"I can't bear to sell you."

207

He pressed himself against it in as close an embrace as anyone could get with a piece of metal and took comfort in the knowledge that he had written his will to take care of its future. When his breath began to condense onto the window, he pulled away and toddled down to his front door, going inside without a glance back.

CHAPTER TWENTY EIGHT

"Mrs Edwards. Not sure if you remember me?"

The woman was clearly quite old but her eyes had the sharpness of an inquisitor.

"Yes, of course I do," she replied, showing irritation at his doubt. "You came that day I found Joe."

"Yes," Richie affirmed.

"Well, how is he?" she demanded.

Richie hesitated as his words caught in his throat. "Could I come in?" he asked eventually.

The woman glanced behind her like she had some enormous secret hidden in her hallway. "Yes, I suppose so."

Richie made his way into a very neat drawing room, immaculate in its tidy sanitation. He felt awkward about sitting down as the chairs looked as if they'd been ironed smooth. She gestured sharply with a pointed finger so he obliged, perching on the edge.

"Thank you," he said in a whisper that fitted with the museum like atmosphere.

She waited for him to speak, her face squeezed as tight as a shrivelled lemon. He chewed a finger, half expecting to be told off.

"I'm afraid...."

That he could not complete the sentence was not through fear of upsetting her, but because it sounded so final and drew an unwelcome solid line between himself and the past.

"He's died," she said, without feeling.

"Yes," he mumbled.

She drew breath in, then let it out with a roll of her lips, the information thus processed.

"Well, I'm surprised he lasted as long as he did. I thought he was gone when I saw him sprawled out on the kitchen floor."

Richie frowned, not enjoying the image she had planted in his head. "He never recovered, really."

"So I heard."

"Did you not go and see him?"

"Oh no. I hate those homes, full of living corpses."

Richie saw her sitting so upright in her own mausoleum and shrugged at the irony. "I suppose. I could never get any reaction from him."

"Well, there you are," she said, justifying her point.

"I was glad I went," Richie countered, folding his hands under his chin while he recalled Joe in his magnolia room, attended by nurses in green bibs and hushed plastic shoes. "His eyes were always open. I'm sure he could see, he just couldn't communicate. Then I thought it was deliberate, like he was on permanent pause, shutting out all of life while he waited for the end."

Mrs Edwards appeared alarmed by this level of detail and clutched her chunky necklace. Richie wondered if she had an ejector button hidden in the central diamond, ready to fire him off if he carried on much more.

"So he left everything to you?"

"Well, yes, the property. There's wasn't much else."

"Are *you* moving in to his bungalow? she enquired with a hint of distaste.

"Err, no. We, my wife and I....she wouldn't want to move down here, not lively enough for her."

Richie realised this could be taken as an insult. Before he could clarify his statement she spoke again.

"The property went on the market eight months ago."

"Sold now, before he....passed on. I've got the job of clearing his stuff. There were no relatives to speak of."

"So you'll be taking that car away?"

"Yes, yes. He left it to me, too."

She looked at him with much pity. "A piece of junk. It was rotting away before he collapsed, must have been three years it never went out. After almost another and all the damp weather we had this last winter, it's turned green with mould. What an eyesore. I can see it from my kitchen window, you know."

"Sorry," Richie said.

She gave him a look plastered with pity. "Now you get the cost of disposing of it."

Richie bristled. "I'm going to keep it," he announced. This was news to himself as much as to her.

"No one in their right mind would want that old thing," she decided, as if he wasn't in the room.

"It has sentimental value. I owned it myself once, a long time ago."

"I wish you luck," she said, standing to indicate the end of his visit.

He departed quickly, pausing only once he was back outside. "I'm grateful to you for looking out for him."

"Oh, he was never any bother. He kept himself to himself mostly. And forever tinkering with that car."

Hearing about Joe's life made Richie become wistful again. "He visited me a few times to begin with, then that became an occasional letter. It was just a Christmas card in the end, with a bit of scribbled news. I should have taken some time to come see him. Life got busy, with the kids and everything."

"All things fade away," she said without a trace of emotion in her powdered face.

Richie nodded and stumbled as he walked away. She would be watching his every move. He fumbled for Joe's key, hurrying inside with the weight of sadness hanging awkwardly around his neck.

~

Richie found sorting through Joe's things easier than his mother's. He had never known the man that well. Whether obvious or hidden, each little part of his life had no more relevance than boot fair fodder. There were a lot books and records, overflowing from the shelves and arranged in leaning piles of no discernible order. He clearly liked cooking, judging by the number of pots and pans in the kitchen. He decorated the walls with pictures of mythology, a theme that ran on through all the ornaments. Only when he found a copy of his mother's funeral service in a drawer, kept flat under a telephone directory, did he react with anything more than a wistful smile. It brought into focus the enduring connection between Joe and his mum, cemented in less than twenty four hours yet lasting decades. Now Joe became a sad, lonely figure, preserving a memory like a beautiful melody that never became a song. With his passing it was gone.   All that was left of the two of them was the car.

Richie had spent the better part of two days at the bungalow, returning to his hotel to sleep and eat, making trips to the local waste centre and charity shops, without going anywhere near the Jensen.

It crouched at the end of the stony track, sheltered, camouflaged, the apparent slumber a bluff ready to catch him cold. He put off going up there, always finding something else that needed packing away. When he had emptied the wardrobe, with Joe's clothes all bundled up in a neat row of black sacks, he sat on the bed and tried to rationalise his anxiety.

The last time he had sat in that beast of a vehicle was when he had fled from Siena in an attempt to leave behind his stupidity. His heart had bled that day. How often had he thought of Alessia and what might have been? Even more so of late, in the quiet cold of a fading marriage.

Oh, to be that young again, and in love. Why did he find everything so difficult? He knew nothing of how hard life could hit you. His best years had been stolen from him while he endeavoured to find out who he was. It created a person he was not comfortable with, lost in pretence and lies.

212

"I must go and face an old friend," he said to the fingers he was chewing. He located the keys. Joe had put them on a fob that had Carol written in gold letters. Even now, it remained his mother's pride and joy. He must approach with caution.

He froze before he reached the bonnet, his feet rooted to the ground, chest tight, mouth dry. It looked so dilapidated. A metaphor for his past, the crumbled remains a reminder that all last chances were gone. Pathetic and wretched, something built for speed and show rusting in a heap, unable to run any more. The first detail he noticed was the mould. On the sun roof, the sides, the hubs, the radiator grill. A brown, green film of suffocating slime covered places where the beautiful light used to sparkle. Dull silver was flecked with brown. The entire chassis sank towards the front left corner, let down by a completely deflated tyre.

Richie plucked up the courage to put the key in the lock. It made a gravelly, crunching sound before the catch popped. The door swung open and there were the controls, coated with dust but still keeping their spaceship potency. He sat in, the leather of the seats lacking the softness he remembered.

He felt a strange affinity with the car. Their separate journeys to this point had left them both battered and tired, a pale shadow of former glory. The world had finally worn them down. Patches of water had pooled onto the dashboard and foot wells, leaking in from above.

With curiosity he gave the engine a try. All he got was an empty, coughing sound, spewing out through clogged carburettors, pitiful as a dying man who has spent too long in the coal mine. All the mighty dials before him sat resolutely at zero, refusing to move.

He sat on out there for a while, patting the lifeless steering wheel. His mind went back to his mother on her deathbed, and to Joe. They suffered this same fate, unable to move, fighting for breath, their fire gone cold. Time saw to that. Except the Jensen was different, you could bring it back if you

213

had the willpower. And plenty of money. You could cruise in power and luxury once again. He jumped out and made his way back to the bungalow. At the fence by the door he found Mrs Edwards, intent on gathering information.

"How are you getting on?" she asked in a falsely light tone.

"Okay," Richie replied. "It's hard. There's a lot of stuff he's accumulated."

"You're not getting any help?"

"No."

"Your wife not free?"

Richie shrugged. "She has to work."

"Well its Friday. Hopefully she'll join you for the weekend."

He stared into the overgrown grass between them and tried to imagine her making such a gesture.

"We'll see," he said, smiling only on one side of his mouth.

"Perhaps one of your children will offer some help."

"They're too busy with their own things."

He had stopped with his hand resting on the handle. Mrs Edwards's eyes flashed expectantly, waiting to catch a glimpse inside.

"You know, I need to check the garden shed," he lied. "Excuse me."

He walked off round the side of the building, leaving her frustrated. There, he found an old bench and sat, watching the sun drift below the tree line, until a cool breeze stole in and made him shiver in the half light.

CHAPTER TWENTY NINE

Richie had Sheryl Crow for company that Saturday night, singing bright and hopeful. He'd found the album amongst Joe's collection, put it on and turned the sound up loud when he began to feel freed from the melancholy. He joined in on lead vocals, picturing her in the video performing on the street with a short skirt and great skin. He was as up as he'd been for months, until his wife arrived.

She deflected his attempt at a kiss when she strode on into the lounge. Sheryl was still having fun, loudly. His wife went over to the stereo and turned the music right down.

Richie felt suddenly small. "That was our song, remember, back in '94," he said.

She looked at him blankly, her long hair making her face appear thin. She shook her head.

"Well, I do," he continued, picking up the sleeve from the top of a pile and admiring the artwork. "I want it played at my funeral."

"How depressing," she said.

"It's been a bit like that of late," he muttered, glancing around him.

She followed suit, taking in the heaps of his efforts. He took the opportunity to assess her properly. He saw her slender frame, leaner than ever of late, swamped by an oversized jumper. The line of her brow was straight, serious, and matched the mouth below it, unyielding and firm. She seemed restless, her feet not settling.

"There's lots here," she commented.

"It's good to see you, Michelle, I've missed you."

He took a step forward and she stopped twisting and stood still, challenging him with the emptiness in her eyes. His advance immediately ceased.

"I slept here last night, got fed up with trekking back and forth to the hotel."

She nodded, plunging her hands into pockets hidden by her baggy jumper.

"I was going to do the same tonight. You can join me. I've got a bottle of wine in the fridge, we can sit up talking."

"We do need to talk," she said, gravely.

"You're right. We do. There's so much I want to talk about."

The unexpected tone of his enthusiasm hung in the air between them. He knew they were likely to have different objectives. False hope, for him, was better than no hope at all. He waited for confirmation from her that she would stay. Michelle displayed the same disdain she had maintained for him for years, her head tilted to one side like a school teacher listening to an incorrect answer.

"The oven works, I can cook pizza," he added, despite realising that pepperoni and mozzarella alone would not be enough to convince her.

"Richie, we need to start working things out."

"Agreed. I'll get cooking."

~

So he put together a mini feast, trying all the while to allude to happier days they had spent together, while she constantly changed the subject to recent times and the enjoyable things she'd been doing without him. They sat on the floor, apart, amongst the accumulated junk of someone else's life and set about sorting out their own.

"Heard much from the kids?" he enquired.

"The odd message, mostly frivolous. They're young. They still believe in laughter and relationships."

Richie took a big gulp of wine to prevent him reacting. He held on to a fantasy, one that included Michelle as carefree lover, the lead part in his story. The reality here was a very pale version. Her jaded demeanour frightened him.

"I thought we could use this enforced break to make some decisions," she said.

"And what have you concluded?" he asked, wincing inwardly in anticipation.

216

"That I like my independence. And even though you've been sleeping in the spare room for six months and we've barely spoken in that time, it felt good to have you properly out of the way."

"Oh."

His response was tiny, crushed. A small boy stung by a large bee and no one to run to. He ran his fingers across the carpet, which was rough and worn.

"You're surprised?" she exclaimed.

"Disappointed," he said. "To hear you say that."

"Holy shit! Richie, It's as much as I've been capable of to hold myself together."

The force behind her words sent him into retreat. His impassive face did not reveal the disquiet inside.

Michelle was tight, her limbs rigid as they expressed frustration. "It takes a lot to understand you," she hissed.

"Does it?"

"Aaagh!" she cried. "I tell you what, you explain to me what you want and I'll go from there."

"I want to start again."

"Start? From where?"

Richie stood up. "The beginning. Me. As a new person. Not that complicated idiot, never satisfied, but as the right man for you. No more fanciful ideas about what might be. Real stuff, right in front of you, every day worth something for what it is."

Michelle was unmoved by his Shakespeare-esque soliloquy. "So how do you propose to make that possible? Leopards have spots for a reason; a hunter will always be a hunter."

Richie was perturbed by her insight. He searched the empty walls for the bubbling optimism he had generated here. Perhaps if he put Sheryl on again?

"What you've been is what you are," she pronounced in syllables icy enough to freeze any dream.

He turned away and went over the curtained window that faced towards the back.

Without facing her he formalised his intentions. "I want to get that car going again. Maybe if I can do that I can restart myself too."

Michelle's laugh made him drive the idea further into the light. He came back to sit on the floor in front of her, dropping down quickly with renewed energy.

"I'm going to use some of the money from the sale of this place to repair the Jensen. And once it's done I'm going to take us all over Europe, to all those romantic places we used to list before we had children."

"Really?" she scoffed. "When have you ever delivered on any of your schemes?"

"This time," he asserted, swinging his clenched fist into a pile of books.

"Mr Prapslater," she said. "That's what the kids call you. Always perhaps later."

"This time," he repeated. "I've sat out in it, I can feel the strength at the wheel. The strength I need."

She stood now, high above, rigid as a statue, hands on hips, her chin thrust towards him in contempt. "Well if you do as you say it will only be to impress the girls."

"Rubbish!"

"Fancy another like the last one, barely out of school and as gullible as hell?"

"No!"

"Or someone from work again. Remember Debbie? She understands me, you told me. Had big tits more like."

"Don't do this now," Richie pleaded.

218

Michelle's sarcasm was unbridled. "Oh, so sorry. Too uncomfortable for you?"

"It's in the past!" he snapped.

"Which you can't change," she argued, with a clever smile.

"I can try."

"You've got your mother's genes. Remember? She started chasing dreams, got tired of dull suburbia and went shagging across Europe."

Now Richie was riled. "Don't speak about her like that!"

"It's true."

"It's okay for you, with your cosy parents ready to drop everything for you. My mum died. You don't know how hard that is."

"Oh, I do. I had to live with you. Moping about her was one reason you gave for your philandering. That and me becoming dull."

"I'm different now."

"How?"

"Older. Wiser. The thrill of those conquests is gone, for me."

"Forgotten how to shoot? Or afraid they won't notice you any more?"

"My good looks have been worn away by the years."

Her fury cooled as he slumped back into the sofa like a boy left out of the football team. "I guess it's all irrelevant now," she admitted. "We're both old farts."

"But we don't have to be!" Richie exclaimed, the slightest hope galvanising him, bringing him bolt upright in the chair. "You remember me. I brought you out into the world, away from the dark Catholic corners of your dogma-led life. We learned so much, fought so hard, sang the same victorious tune together, got excited about the future. And you taught me mercy and understanding.

"Now you need to find some of your own. If you want to feel those things again, fly out of the cage you've put us in and make it good."

His impassioned plea was pushed away with the leftovers of the pizza she shoved with her foot across the carpet.

"Sorry, Richie. I can't just forget how you let me down. I'm going to sleep in the bedroom. You can have the floor in here. Don't come bothering me, I'm not interested. I'm going home first thing in the morning."

Once she had shut herself away, Richie wandered the remains of Joe's existence and considered packing himself in one of the boxes to be taken to the dump. His ravaged mind kept returning to the car out under the collapsing port. That was his way out of this hopeless mess.

He walked up to the blank door she hid behind and pictured her curled up on top of the covers. How dearly he wanted to go in and curl himself up against her bony frame, to drain away the spite he had allowed to develop.

"I'm gonna make that car perfect," he called out. "For mum, for Joe, and for me."

"Fine," came the reply. "Just don't be too sure I'll be there to see it."

CHAPTER THIRTY

"So this is the famous Jensen Interceptor."

Richie pushed the protective goggles up onto the top of his head to find his son standing in the mouth of the garage.

"Hey, Danny," Richie cried. "Good to see you!"

He went to give him a hug but with the reserve of strangers it became a handshake. From this distance they could check each other out. Richie always saw Danny as a harder version of himself. He had the same strong cheekbones and flat temples. Michelle's stern looks showed up in his tightly drawn mouth, giving him an air of meanness. He was scruffy in jeans and a t-shirt that needed a good wash.

"Student life treating you well?" Richie asked.

Danny shrugged. "Can't complain. It's my final year, I'll have to work hard."

"Finally," Richie said.

Danny caught his obvious humour. "Yeah, less games, more study."

"You could do with a haircut," the older man observed.

"You're just jealous because you're losing yours."

Richie ran his hand across his scalp. The floppy style he had sported for so long was gone. "It's having you kids that made this happen," he said.

"Really? I didn't think you hardly noticed us."

They both found this statement difficult to follow. Richie fiddled with his blow torch, his heart pounding so hard he could feel it in his clenched teeth. Danny fidgeted uncomfortably, wondering whether to make a quick exit. The big expanse of the car's bonnet stretching out before them was too much to ignore.

"This is quite a motor, dad," he said.

"Yes, it is."

221

Danny let out a short, embarrassed laugh, like he wasn't sure what to say next.

"Let me show you," Richie urged.

Danny appeared pleased and followed his father eagerly into the garage. They spent some time examining the various parts, stared at the engine and gazed at the many dials. Danny patted the roof, leaned back to take in the dynamics and made all the right impressed noises. He knew very little about cars, Richie recognised that. The important thing was his interest in the whole restoration project and his respect for the historical importance it held for their family.

"You told us a lot of stories about your mum and how buying this changed her," Danny said, sitting in the passenger seat beside Richie, who gripped the steering wheel and imagined himself back on the cobbles of Siena on a hot afternoon.

"And they were all true," Richie said with a nostalgic smile. "Or mostly all."

"I wish I could have met her. It would have been so cool to have a hippy granny like that."

"She lived on the edge in those days. But I still felt she looked out for me."

"Like a parent should."

Richie cracked at this point. "Look. I know I wasn't around much when you were having trouble at school. Working away doesn't help your relationships. I went through something similar when my mother went away. I was eleven. It's part of growing up, some of us have to do it quicker than others."

Danny gazed off out of the windscreen, his face red. Richie was sure he wanted to say something and couldn't work out whether it would help or not. While the boy wrestled with his thoughts, Richie tried a different plea.

"Your mum coped amazingly with me not being there–"

"And the rest," Danny added, turning on his father.

Richie had looked at the same eyes in the mirror many times and not found solace.

"Okay. Everything I got up to she dealt with. For your sake, and your sister's. She is an angel and she watched over you."

Danny smiled at this notion. Richie smiled too. Every man found the blanket of maternal love reassuring.

"I bet she's been fussing since you arrived back," Richie said.

Danny laughed. "Just a bit. Once I'd been told off for not having a coat. It was a relief to come out here. I thought she was going to start washing behind my ears."

"Or cleaning your nails!"

They chuckled in unison and tension was banished.

"So she says you've been obsessed with working on the car since they towed it here."

"I've surprised myself," Richie admitted. "I bought a manual, tracked some replacement parts online, got the right tools and barring the odd mistake I'm making progress. I'm really enjoying the challenge. It's the most energy I've had in ages."

"I think you're doing a good job," Danny said.

Richie knew his son could have little comprehension of what constituted 'a good job'. Danny was really alluding his father's newfound endeavour and patted the dashboard as a sign of approval.

"There's a small dent here," he observed.

"Yes, I'm aware. It was there since before mum had it. I've always been curious about that."

"Something bad?" Danny wondered.

"Maybe."

"Doesn't matter. A small detail. The whole thing is amazing."

"There was a lot of rust and mould to get rid of. The guy who'd had it became too old."

"I know. Was he really your mum's lover?"

"Yes."

223

"Wow. And she bought it at an auction?"

"Yes."

"Cool."

He twisted round to take in the back and ran his hands along the window ledges. "I was mad on racing cars when I was young," he said.

"I remember."

"You do?"

Richie gave him a look that needed no further discussion.

Danny moved on. "I kind of lost interest once I discovered beer."

"And girls."

Danny admitted as much with a nod.

"I'll let you drive this once it's ready," Richie told him.

"Okay," Danny agreed with a gulp.

"Keep the family link going."

Michelle appeared in the garage entrance, silhouetted by the afternoon sun. It was not possible to see her face. She disappeared again.

"Are we in trouble?" Richie speculated.

"No!" Danny exclaimed. "Not us."

They exchanged a glance of uncertainty.

"However," Danny continued. "I don't know about you, but I'm starving. I could smell one of her casseroles when I arrived. Shall we go and see if it's ready?"

"Good plan," Richie said, and together they went inside to the family dining table.

~

"Well, here's to us. And the absent daughter."

Richie held his glass of wine aloft. Danny followed suit, all be it with less of a flourish. Michelle did not respond and began picking at her dinner.

"It's a shame that Miranda can't be here," Richie continued.

"She has to work," Michelle reminded him without even glancing up.

224

Despite the spaciousness of the room, there was a claustrophobic feel that wrapped them in too closely.

"She hasn't made it home since Easter," Richie said.

"I wonder why?" Michelle wondered with mock innocence. "Can you think of a reason, Danny?"

"Mum, don't involve me in this," he asked.

"But you are involved. This is a family. Or was."

Richie frowned. "Shall we just enjoy the food, Michey." She showed distaste at his use of her pet name. He carried on regardless. "This is a great pot roast, my love."

"Oh yes. Let's keep playing the game," she retorted in a sweet voice. Richie could not match her when she went on the offensive. Her features pulled tight and shoulders hunched. At times like this he was amazed that he ever had the courage to be unfaithful to her.

"So are you still sharing accommodation with the same two guys?" he asked Danny.

They went off into a discussion about his daily routines. Michelle plodded on silently, shaking her head in frustration, a gesture Richie caught in the corner of his eye. Since the Jensen had arrived he had tried to keep a low profile, hoping time would allow their wounds to heal. He remembered her gentleness and wished every night that she might come to his bed seeking relief.

"Mum, would you mind if I dashed? A few old friends are meeting up at the Holly Bush. I'd like to catch up with them."

"Stay for dessert," Richie implored.

"Of course you can go. Take the key from the peg, come back when you want just don't be noisy."

He got up and looked nervously at one parent and then the other. "Try and be nice to each other," he encouraged.

"Have fun," Richie called to him as he left.

225

Silence fell as a heavy, wet blanket on the two left behind. Face to face, each of them toyed with the remains of their dinner, the chink of cutlery on china sounding like a padlock on a cage.

"We should do as he says," Richie suggested lightly.

"What's that?" Michelle asked, her mind clearly elsewhere.

"Be nice to each other."

She laughed so harshly Richie could take no pleasure in her amusement.

"Not a hope," she stated.

"We used to be good at it."

"Along with a lot of other things."

"So we can be again."

"Don't start that again."

"But we could."

"I'm not so sure. I think all that's left are the shadows of how it was." Her eyes made no contact with his. She followed herself through the labyrinth of a broken past without any expectation of ever emerging. However brightly his beacon might be, beckoning her through, she would not see it if she didn't look up.

"You were wrong to try and bring Danny into it," he said, as much as anything to get a reaction. She did not disappoint.

"He's always been part of it. Miranda too. They felt let down as well. While you were chasing Debbie and whoever else, you weren't paying attention to them. There's more to being a family than a game of Cluedo at Christmas!"

"I provided for them!" he cried.

"Terrific!" she spat. "What Miranda needed was you at the hospital bedside just once in all her admissions. She knows you paid for the best care, probably saved her. But she idolised you for years until she gave up waiting for the touch of your hand when she needed it."

226

Richie leapt up, knocking the chair back with a clatter across the parquet flooring. Now Michelle looked at him, saw him clench his fists and shake them at the ceiling.

"Okay. I get it! I was no great father. But that is in the past. They're not children any more, they're not here anymore. It's just us. Now we can either work together or go our separate ways.

"Just be certain about what you decide. I love you, I can say it to you without flinching. You need to understand that if you walk away from me tonight, I won't ever be able to tell you that again. And that would be tragic, because I've seen how much you care for me. You notice what I do, when I walk past, you clock my feelings. You don't bother with such things if the hope has really gone."

There was a considerable pause while Richie, breathless with emotion, waited for a reaction, a response, one tiny spark of optimism in the dying embers of their marriage. He watched her like an accused might view a jury, trying to read every thought. Her expression remained a blank canvas, ready to reveal the dramatic scene behind.

"Sit down, Richie. I'll fetch the dessert."

So, on opposite sides of the table where they had previously held a thousand family feasts, a couple shared a sticky toffee pudding with custard and spoke no more about all the mistakes they had made.

CHAPTER THIRTY ONE

The evening came on cold, the chill creeping into the wide garage where Richie was working. He'd keep on going until his fingers got too stiff to be useful. It was better than being in the house facing the threat of criticism for everything he was, and had been. It got lonely as the hours stretched out, the radio crackling from the high shelf offering the only company, apart from a regular visit from a mouse, which had the uncanny habit of stopping to stare at him, with its nose twitching with curiosity. Even the rodents thought he was odd. But the time he was putting in was paying dividends. The Jensen had begun to shine again, the radiator held the grin of a prisoner coming to the end of their confinement. Richie would stop now on occasions and just sit in the driver's seat and let his imagination drive off. He'd be young, with his arm wrapped around a beautiful girl's slim, bare shoulders while his other hand steered the car into a sunset of fire. Maybe it was Spain. It didn't really matter. She only had eyes for him and kisses that were a call to action. This was a fantasy, not Alessia. Something separate and new, where he was free from mistakes and bad judgement.

It was a shame to come back to his little corner of suburbia where self-loathing hid in the underbelly of comfort. All the work he had put in was unlikely to change his situation. He knew he had to face up to losing Michelle. She might just leave any day now, although he sensed she was waiting to see what he did next, or was he just imagining it? Either way, he had began to slow, putting off finishing the project and having nothing left to get up for.

On this night he completed the seal on the sun roof and when he stepped away he knew this was the final piece in the fragile jigsaw. Apart from a good wax and polish, it was done. If he thought he would have felt elated he was disappointed. Sliding his tools back into the box and closing the lid was a small thing that held a massive consequence. This had been a journey to a final set of crossroads. Judgement day had arrived.

Outside the garage he paused and looked up. The immensity of dark sky overwhelmed him. Between the many twinkling stars that had so inspired his mother, he sought for the umpteenth time some kind of answer, a trace of her he could recognise. As usual, he was left unrewarded, his eyes dewy with disappointment.

When he went into the house, there was deathly silence. Everywhere was tidy and measured, as if troubles could be shut away, unseen, nonexistent. Only the warm smell of baking in the kitchen betrayed the trace of life. He smiled, reminded of the times when his mother still cooked for the household. He had not come to dinner, nor been invited. He wondered if Michelle was actually there at all. Perhaps she had made a quick getaway? The closed door to the bedroom was a firm reminder that she was at home, just not available.

As he climbed into his own bed, he pulled the covers up tight under his chin. All the promises he had shattered came back to taunt him in the darkness. He could only hide for so long. Living this way had to come to an end. He resolved to load up the car the next day and head off, like his mother had before him, and see where the road might lead him. Maybe he'd find another version of himself that he was happy to be with in the night.

~

The next morning was like so many others. There was no sign of Michelle. He breakfasted alone and headed out to the garage where he checked the car over and set about polishing the paintwork. The iridescent blue came into its own. The colour of a tropical ocean on the perfect day or the sky above an icy mountain peak when the air was fresh and clear.

With a concerted effort he could see his own face reflecting back at him. It looked old, haunted, lonely. And then there was another, a familiar one, beside his, features he knew and trusted. She was an angel.

229

"I brought you a snack," she said.

Richie was startled by the sudden voice and the fact that it was his wife's.

He turned to face cheese sandwiches, a plate of jammy dodgers, and a pot of coffee.

"My favourites," he observed, his tone quizzical with shock.

"I know. I haven't forgotten everything about you."

"Thanks," he said.

When he noticed the two cups she explained. "I brought enough for us both. If you don't mind me joining you out here."

"Of course not!" he cried. "Let me clear some space."

He moved some stuff off the old bench and gestured for her to join him. She seemed faintly amused as they sat beside one another, their legs dangling beneath them like a couple of kids on swings who had stopped to watch the world for a while.

"I bought you this on the first Christmas we moved to this house," she said, patting the faded wood between them. "You had nothing else out here back then."

He was touched that she recalled this detail. He looked at her face to see if he could recognise some of her former affection. She remained in her own place, playing out the memory in the space before her.

"I remember it well."

They ate in silence for a while, the beautifully sleek Jensen stretched out before them, waiting for its moment. The trapped air of the workspace smelt of engine oil. When it came to the time to speak again they did so without turning their gaze from the car.

"You've finished haven't you?" she said.

"Yes."

"I know you're planning to leave."

"Oh."

"I saw your suitcase through the door while I was hovering."

230

"Ah."

"That's why I thought I'd bring out the lunch. I wanted our last hours together to be nice."

"I see."

They each chewed a few sweet biscuits and watched the light go dull when a cloud obscured the sunlight outside the garage.

"I so didn't want to end up the same as my father, everyone left him eventually," Richie mused. "Now it seems I've failed. I wanted to forget the pain of losing mum so I focused on my career, just like my old man. Now I'll be alone having lost the love of my partner and the respect of my children. Out of touch and without direction."

"You have time to change that," she said.

"Time has raced by. It's all gone."

"Not all."

He leaned back so that he was virtually behind her. He wanted to reach out and run his hand down the soft wool of her thin jumper.

"I had no intention of hurting you," he admitted.

"So you've said a hundred times."

"I love you the same now as I ever did."

"You mean, badly."

This made him chuckle out loud. She turned her head, her eyebrow arching over her shoulder.

"That's funny?" she wondered.

"Oh, come on. I know you well enough. You can see the humour in your acid wit."

She hung her head back and contemplated the rough ceiling. "Yes, I guess you have to laugh at us. We've endured this for too long."

He touched her hair gently enough so that she would not be aware. "Why don't you come out for a drive with me?"

231

She sighed and he watched her ribcage rise and fall. "Why would I do that?"

"Because I want you to."

"That's not a reason for me."

"Do you need one?"

"I...."

She did not complete this sentence. Instead, for no definable purpose, she looked at her watch.

"Somewhere else to be?" Richie asked.

"No," she replied. "I've got nowhere to be."

"So please take a ride with me?"

She did not respond. The breathing continued, maybe slightly faster. The mouse came back out from behind the shelving and settled in to wait for a final answer, shaking as much as Richie was. When Michelle sank forward he feared the worse.

"It's a shame," she said.

"What is?"

"That I still love you."

Richie was uncertain how to take this. He chewed nervously on one of his chewed fingers, tasting wax on his tongue. His leg, which had been twitching, upped the rate of involuntary movement.

Michelle got to her feet, picked up the tray and went. She stopped by the front wing of the car and looked across the ocean of bonnet.

"I'll be ready in an hour," she told him and left.

~

"Madam," Richie purred, opening the passenger door for Michelle when she returned.

Her smile was brief and demure as she nodded her acceptance of his chivalry, tucking her dress beneath her as she sat in. The glossy sheen to her hair took away the thinness of her face. A ghost of a memory struck

232

Richie. Siena, 1990, Alessia, when it mattered how everything looked. He'd waited so long to have that emotion again. Here again was a woman in red who had spent time to make herself beautiful, for him to take on a drive in his car.

He rushed around the other side, eager to get started. With crossed fingers and his tongue squashed between his teeth, he turned the key. With a resounding roar, the engine rose and stretched its wings.

"Sounds good," she said, with a grin.

Richie sat up straight, full of pride. All the months and money had achieved something. Michelle caught a glimpse of the young man she had first been drawn to. Boyish, eager to achieve, energetic.

"I see we have company," she remarked, nodding in the direction of the back seat.

His mother's teddy sat there, resolutely cheerful. "He belongs in here," he explained.

"She would be pleased, I'm sure."

An image of Carol filled his mind. Her head resting against his one late afternoon towards the end, mumbling idly about the streets of Siena and the noise the wheels made on the cobbles. A memory that always burst out of the place he kept it. He could not keep it hidden. Michelle could see it, written across his face.

He drew in a deep breath and let the Jensen roll down the drive, his eyes wide with disbelief. They were going forwards. Despite the shake that went through his arms and legs, he was able to make their departure smooth. It was only a short distance from the bland unity of their estate to a fast straight road that led north to open countryside.

The morning rain had faded, the sunshine breaking through to give all the colours a brighter hue. Richie felt charged with the power of the car. The blood pumped through his veins just like the oil and fuel burning hot for the engine.

233

He glanced at Michelle, catching her in profile, noble yet sad, the mascara laden lashes closed. With hands neatly folded in her lap, she appeared to be absorbing every aspect on this one and only journey in this notorious car. His nostrils flared. She was wearing that perfume he loved.

"How well it goes," she said. "Such effortlessness and speed."

He revelled in the moment. The young Richie within emerged, a brilliant orange phoenix in flame, flying above a black and white world. The angel beside him had finally forgotten his sins, absolving him of all crimes. This was the dream, a magic movie moment where every piece fell neatly into place. He was the star.

And then as many champions had before him, he began to make some sense of his triumph. The riches he had reached were his to lose; the trophy would slip through his fingers. Gravity would always win, bringing yet another Icarus back to ground with a nasty crash. A perfect paper aeroplane nose–diving after a loop–de–loop.

Under the burden of his dark fate, he drove on, expecting her to want him to stop somewhere where they could have their climactic chat. When she showed no such inclination he had to re–think. He checked the fuel gauge. Presuming it was reliable he could go for at least another hour. Should they keep on moving? What were her motives for coming with him?

Inspiration came from a direction sign. He turned and took them to a picturesque pub on a green. This was not some random place. It was here, some twenty five years ago, that they met up for their first date.

"Fancy a drink?" he asked, casually, even though he was trembling.

She looked at him and folded her arms. "You chose here specifically?"

"Kind of."

"Why not," she agreed after a little more deliberation. "It *is* apt."

They chose to sit outside, the Jensen nearby as if it were trying to hear where their dialogue took them. It would be disappointed, for they hardly spoke. Richie leaned back and watched the swifts screech by in manic

234

chase, while he avoided Michelle's piercing gaze. She was sizing up the situation, ready for vengeance and without fear.

The sun dipped, sending blades of golden light onto the vast bonnet of the car, slicing between the odd couple and illuminating their differences. One so measured, holding the wrongs of the past as a weapon, the other vague, holding new hope as a shield. Love long lost in the void between.

On the edge of the field opposite, sheep hurried away as the mist gathered by the tree line. Gradually, the atmosphere was giving in to autumn, the cold air creeping stealthily between the warm pockets of summer. Richie shivered.

"Cold?" Michelle asked.

"A bit."

"Time to head back," she said, more as a command than a suggestion.

A crow settled on the fence nearby, cawing noisily what sounded like "Goodbye, good luck!" as the two of them crunched across the gravel.

"So what was that about?" Michelle enquired while she pulled her seat belt on.

"How do you mean?"

"The stop here. Were you trying to make me feel nostalgic?"

"Possibly," Richie admitted, leaning forward against the steering wheel, waiting for her condemnation. "It kind of takes us full circle."

"Back to the same point?"

"Partly. But a new lap."

"Feels like the end of one long, twisty road."

"Right," Richie said, bringing the beast back rumbling to life.

While he manoeuvred out, she cast her eyes around within, hair shaking as her head turned. "You know, now I've finally ridden inside this car, it is a lot better than I thought."

"That's good," he chirped.

"There's a cosiness. I think it likes people."

235

"Really?" Richie said, in some doubt. "I'm less sure, but ready to learn."

"By driving away."

"It's made to take you places."

"Danny said you promised him a drive when he's next back, which would be Christmas now. You can't do that if you've left."

"I don't have to go straight away."

"Why wait, it's what you want to do, isn't it?"

"Yes," he admitted. "Whatever my mum got from her years travelling, I'd like to experience that. I guess I'm still following her dream."

"We haven't spoken about this for such a long time."

His head dropped. "We haven't spoken about a lot of things for a long time."

"The hurt."

"And the healing."

Not knowing why, his attention was drawn to the sizeable dent in the dashboard in front of Michelle's skinny knees. Great suffering could come and go in an instant. The Jensen brought maximum potential for dread as well as optimism. You needed courage to take the trip.

"Watch out!" Michelle screamed.

Richie looked up to see the road veering round to the right while he was going straight on towards a sturdy fence. With surprising agility he corrected their line and brought the car around the corner, tipping onto two wheels and shuddering back to four.

"Sorry," he said.

"You did well," she assured him.

"No, it was you. You saved us from disaster."

He reached down to drop a gear while he stilled his racing heart. The stick was smooth under his sweaty fingers. As he gripped harder, she reached out her hand and laid it on top of his, gripping hard until his knuckles pressed into her palm.

236

They looked at one another and exchanged the kind of smile that can only pass between two people who shared a common past. Two people on a journey. And the magnificent car sped on, relentlessly pulling the occupants to the next part of their story.

CHAPTER THIRTY TWO

He saw it shining like a beacon, blue and silver, metallic, magnetic, drawing him nearer, telling him he needed to get up close. Unfortunately his mother had a tight grip on his hand, wary of his constant wanderings. They were passing by, his chance was going too.

Summoning full strength, he pulled free and ran to where it waited, pleased to have drawn in another admirer. He took a full breath and gently touched the wing. The heat of the sun had charged the polished surface. Electricity ran through his fingers and into his body. This vehicle gave him superpowers. His mum would be no match as she came up to him with an expression sterner than her fair features should ever allow.

"Jonnie, you bad boy. You mustn't ever run off like that!"

"Mum, I had to see this."

She shrugged. "It's just a dull old car," she said.

"No. Not dull. A racer."

"Whatever, let's go."

"No."

She tutted. "Baby, you're way too young to drive."

"Look at how long it is, mum. And what big wheels!"

He left her standing there while he went all the way round to look in through the driver's window. He was only just big enough to see inside.

"Wow! So many dials! I bet it goes so fast!"

"Speed's not everything little man."

He turned his head on one side to gaze up at his mother. She let out a bored yawn out of that pretty mouth, like she often did in the afternoons while he sat at the table and wrote stories from his imagination. Police chases, dragons soaring, a lovely house in a forest and a knight with a big sword coming out of the mist. She never thought about stuff like that. The only time she got animated was when her phone lit up with another

238

message, which didn't always work because she'd throw it back down sometimes with a snarl. He wanted to share his excitement.

"Mum, don't you see. This car has lots to tell us. A hundred stories. Listen."

He put his head against the door. She glanced around nervously. "Careful, honey. These things are expensive."

"Copy me," he insisted.

Reluctantly, for an easier life, she followed suit. She thought she could make out voices. She strained to get them to become clearer. Then she shook her head, blonde hair dancing. It was just the noise of the breeze. But all the time, Jonnie was grinning with the teeth he had, his big eyes moving from side to side as he listened. He laughed out loud, then frowned, nodded and ended with tears welling up.

"What could *you* hear?" she demanded anxiously as he stumbled across to her for a hug.

"So many different things," he told her, with his bony chin pressed into her shoulder. "I could see them too."

"Like what?"

"An open road going to a city of gold, a cage, darkness like death, a crash with lots of blood and glass, another road to....nowhere. Two sad people, another two happy. And always the big roar of an engine."

She held him where she could look into his face. He had sounded like someone else for a moment there. He was serious and very definite.

"Are you okay?"

"Oh, yes, mummy. I'm perfectly fine."

She was less sure, a little spooked. "Well, when you get home you can write down all these stories."

This thought brightened his demeanour. "Oh yes, I will."

"And maybe one day when you sell lots of books you can buy one of these big old cars and take me for a ride."

"And I'll have my own tale to tell," he said, beaming as brightly as the Jensen beside him.

For more information about me and my books please go to my main website

www.chriscloake.co.uk

Alternatively use

www.booklaunch.io/crc44

I hope you have enjoyed this book. Either way, I would dearly love it if you could leave a short review on any popular site.

Sign up to my mailing list for lots of information and offers on

www.chriscloake.co.uk

OTHER WORKS BY CHRIS CLOAKE

SEVEN DAYS

A single, terrible event unlocks a

series of secrets that tears through a

sleepy village.

In an effort to find answers, one girl

is plagued by guilt and fear as she

uncovers the scars of the past and

the pain of the present.

Central to events are The Falls,

where the water surges with

power and majesty, like truth,

relentless and inescapable.

A PHANTOM OF DELIGHT

This is two stories in one, both tied to
the garden at Hambleside and the
dramatic events that unfold over the
course of ninety years.
Maria keeps a journal that records her
epic struggle for survival in a world
dominated by men and the two wars
they waged.
Violent forces are unleashed that
threaten to destroy her existence and take
away the people she loves. Only the
image of her mother, who she lost at
birth, and the garden her parents created
seem to offer the strength to help.
Chuck, a distant relative from Canada,
arrives having inherited Hambleside.
His own life has broken down and he
discovers, through Maria's incredible
story, a mirror to his own despair and the
challenges lying in wait..
Will the heavy history of Hambleside and
the many dark secrets of the past allow
him the chance of a new beginning?

MOONLIGHT DRIVE

On a moonlight drive I lost my dream. Jill was that dream.
Why did I drive the car so fast? I knew the road was wet. Why did there have to be that big old tree waiting for us on the corner? And why did I live while she died?
Each fine moment keeps coming back to me. Her face, that smile, her skin so soft and eyes so wild.
I wake up to her husband at my bedside, holding my hand and crying. He knows nothing of our love. I will survive, he assures me. I can go home to my wife and children. See my parents again. Go back to my old job. Run and play sport again.
I want none of this. Only Jill. I need to be with her. I need our love. I must escape this pain. I need another moonlight drive.

Printed by Replika Press India Ltd.